One Year of School and *The Island*

OPUNTIA

Opuntia is an imprint of Agincourt Press

Opuntia Books are published by
Luigi Ballerini
Beppe Cavatorta
Gianluca Rizzo
Federica Santini

Agincourt Press is a non-profit chaired by Berardo Paradiso

The publisher wishes to thank
Taylor Bechtel and Emma Freund for their editorial assistance

ISBN: 978-1-946328-29-8

AGINCOURT PRESS
P.O. Box 1039
Cooper Station
New York, NY 10003
www.agincourtpress.org

Giani Stuparich

One Year of School and *The Island*

Translated by
Charles Klopp and Melinda Nelson

Introduction by
Charles Klopp

Preface by
Fulvio Senardi

Agincourt Press
New York, 2021

Table of Contents

Preface

I have often asked Melinda Nelson and Charles Klopp, who have presented us with these translations of one of the most characteristic voices of Triestine
literature, what it was that made them fall in love with this city, which they
continue to visit, delighted every time to find it always the same, with its sharp
edges and gentle curves, its harshness and its kindness. Is it the ocean, the people, the history inscribed in its streets, buildings, and monuments, the prickly ca-
dences of a dialect whose origins are in the Veneto but is etched by history with
foreign locutions? All that, they suggest, and perhaps something more, though
we don't want to delve too much into a secret that they themselves perhaps don't
completely understand--as always happens with great loves. This is the passion
that has driven Nelson and Klopp to Giani Stuparich.

For better or worse, Giani Stuparich epitomizes Trieste. Like the city, he
is a bit old-fashioned, though like the city, he emanates an overwhelming cha-
risma. Of distant Slavic origins (as his last name makes clear) but with Jewish
ties on his mother's side, he attended a German-language elementary school
and then the municipal Italian-language Liceo-Gymnasium. He was thus an
"alloy forged from different races," as he himself wrote in *Trieste as I Remember It* (*Trieste nei miei ricordi*). Stuparich began his intellectual life trying his
hand at history, turning afterwards to narrative, attracted to the challenges of
art rather than those of historical research. His commitment to the past, however, risked taking him along a perilous path during the years of triumphant
Fascism. Art, on the other hand, promised to draw him closer to the mystery of
humankind in a whirlwind of what he called "torment" and "joy." It imposed
the exhausting obligation to keep digging and, when he experienced the mir-
acle of understanding, be rewarded with a kind of "liberation." In *Trieste as
I Remember It,* he describes such an activity as "a tunnel we excavate within
ourselves that opens onto the universe." This is very likely the Stuparich who
is likely to endure; the two stories that Nelson and Klopp have chosen to share

with English-language readers clearly represent the culmination of his abilities as a writer.

Well integrated into the tradition of narrative fiction (he has cited Anton Chekhov and Katherine Mansfield as his most important forerunners), Stuparich is attentive to the innermost configurations of sensibility and character, making use of the tools of pre-Freudian psychology. And he is able, above all, to situate his characters in a "living city" that cannot be detached from them. So we have Stuparich the novelist; Stuparich the apocalyptic author of *Simone;* and Stuparich the bard of the First World War in *They'll Come Back (Ritorneranno)*, a book that was considered outmoded when first printed, an echo of antiquated terms from the distant Nineteenth Century. It may be that this work was, as the critic Bruno Maier thought, a "noble deed" rather than a great novel. Stuparich's diary of his first months in the trenches in 1915, called in fact *Guerra del '15*, occupies a special place in his literary production and is without doubt his masterpiece. Reworked more than he wanted to make it appear, the text is fresh in its impressions and emotions, a voice that rings out in the readers' minds and goes straight to their hearts and consciences. Yes, to their very consciences because Stuparich is a powerfully moral writer, whether as a narrator, a politically committed journalist, or, above all, as a man.

During the years of nationalistic strife his contributions were characterized by moderation and good sense and his decision to support Italy's intervention, when the Great War had already exploded, represented the obligatory choice of someone who feared the Germanization of Europe and of Trieste in particular. He was not fond of Fascism, and his late enrollment in the party in 1940 is the gesture of a someone being blackmailed: the son and the husband of Jewish women, he was more concerned for his daughters than he was for himself during the years marked by the racist laws with which Italy wanted to demonstrate that it was on the same level as Hitler's Germany. After the war he found his beacon in the new democracy of a country that had rediscovered the path traced earlier by social philosopher and activist Giuseppe Mazzini and by the political and military leader Giuseppe Garibaldi. After 1945, Stuparich took up his pen once more to compose cultural and political newspaper articles and opinion pieces. Determined to recommit to the struggle for Trieste's Italian character—for him, an unassailable value—he also remained faithful to the principles of his own individual, tolerant humanism, convinced that culture can serve as a bridge between individuals and peoples.

To this rich and complex writer who has been so unjustly forgotten, despite the splendid rediscovery efforts by the Quodlibet publishing house and the significant critical interest that has been rekindled in regard to his works, Melinda Nelson and Charles Klopp have chosen to commit themselves to him and make Stuparich speak in their language. As an intellectual, a Triestino, and a friend, I can only express my thanks and immense gratitude to them.

Giani Stuparich was born and spent most of his life in Trieste. His first name is a variant of "Gianni," the usual diminutive of "Giovanni," but with the lack of the double letter that is characteristic of Triestino, the dialect or local language of his native city and the preferred means of oral communication for most of its residents even today. The cosmopolitan and fiercely independent Trieste where Stuparich lived and wrote for most of his life underwent dramatic changes in the course of his years there. These changes are mirrored—and in some cases have been defined for posterity—in the pages of his fiction and essays.

At the time of Stuparich's birth in 1891, Trieste was an important, even crucial outlet for the overseas commerce of the Austro-Hungarian empire. But by the time the writer died in Rome in 1961, the city's status as a prosperous commercial emporium had declined significantly. For by this time Trieste was no longer Austrian but Italian and was competing with other Italian outlets to the sea and dependent on Rome for financial support. Before 1918, by contrast, it had been the only warm-water port for a vast and wealthy empire that was looked on with favor by a meticulously bureaucratic but culturally indulgent Vienna intent on maintaining its mercantile profile in the Mediterranean and beyond.

The years when Stuparich lived in Trieste also saw a falling off in the cultural and intellectual life of the city, as compared to the period when Italo Svevo (1861-1928) and Umberto Saba (1883-1957) were writing their fiction and poetry and holding forth in the cafés of the city. Both writers were contemporaries and Svevo, in particular, was a friend of James Joyce, who was also busy in Trieste in the early twentieth century. The Irish writer has even been memorialized with a life-size statue in the city center, as have Svevo and Saba in municipal homage to these three pillars of the city's literary past. Both Svevo and Saba were also friends with Virgilio Giotti (1885-1957), Trieste's greatest poet in the local dialect and a figure of national stature as well. Although Stuparich knew and spent some time as a young man with these (usually) convivial writers, he belongs, in terms of literary history, to the generation that succeeded theirs. When Stuparich published his first collection of stories in 1929, Svevo (who had died the previous year), Saba, and Giotti were already well-established. And Italy, of which Trieste was now a part, was in the grip of Fascism, a political reality that Svevo stayed clear of in his writings and that Giotti and Saba (who, like Svevo, was partly Jewish), were forced to endure only in the later years of their lives.

The generation of writers and thinkers to which Stuparich belonged was acutely conscious of their responsibility to promote the culture of their native city and region. Among this newer generation was Stuparich's close friend, Scipio Slataper. Slataper was born in Trieste in 1888 and died fighting on the Italian side in the First World War. After slipping across the border from Austria into Italy but before he volunteered for military service against the Austrians who ruled the city where he was born, Slataper served as managing editor of the nationally important Florentine journal, *La Voce*, and had begun to make a name for himself as a writer. Slataper's lyrical novel of 1912, *Il mio Carso*—the title is a reference to the rocky plateau that lies above the city—is important for the development of his friend Stuparich's art and thinking because it examines some of the themes and ethical issues that were later to become crucial for Stuparich too. Slataper's perspective on cultural matters was an original one that was strongly influenced by his readings in German and Nordic literatures and bolstered by his sympathies for the Slavs who lived in the region, people Slataper admired for their vitality and thus their promise as agents in a future vivification of the region, even though he was convinced that Trieste should remain culturally Italian. After Slataper's death in the war, Stuparich served as biographer and editor of a number of his friend's writings and, like many others in Trieste who knew their charismatic author, venerated his memory.

The writings produced by the generation of Stuparich, Slataper, and the others was a literature in which patriotism was of great importance. For the young men and women of the city who considered themselves Italian, this patriotism took the form of a nationalist desire for union with an Italy they were convinced was their cultural homeland, even though they had been born legally Austrian. At the same time, like Slataper, many of the Italophonic writers and thinkers of this period were profoundly influenced by the Germanic and, to a lesser extent, the Slavic cultures so unmistakably present in the streets and squares of their native city. Many of these intellectuals, including Alberto Spaini on whom the anagrammatically named Pasini is based in *One Year of School,* went to German-speaking schools or universities, and spoke German as readily as they did Italian or Triestino. Edda Marty, the female protagonist of the novella in which Spaini/Pasini appears, has a German-speaking father and a Slavic mother as well as a sister who is studying at the University of Vienna. And the family into which Virgilio Giotti was born as Virgilio Schönbeck was originally from a German-speaking area. In Giotti's own family, Russian, the native language of the wife he had met during his own sojourn in Florence, was also spoken by the poet and his two sons, both of whom perished fighting as Fascist conscripts in their mother's native country. As for Spaini, after the attempted suicide that inspired the similar gesture that is described in *One Year of School,* he went on to become a noted translator and Germanist. Since there was no university in Trieste, Stuparich himself began his post-secondary education at the University of Prague before transferring to the University of Florence in the same city where he later joined the Italian military. Despite his experiences in localities that were not primarily Italian speaking, including Prague (his first book was called *The Czech Nation* and went through two editions in its author's lifetime), all of Stuparich's writings are written in Italian, and he considered himself an Italian writer, as does literary history since.

When World War I broke out, with Italy joining the hostilities in 1915, Stuparich, along with his younger brother Carlo and many of their friends and classmates including Slataper, joined the fighting on the Italian side. Doing so meant staking their lives on the hope that the city where they had been born and grown up would be united with Italy after a victorious conclusion to the war, which did happen, though with certain economically deleterious results the young enthusiasts had not entirely foreseen. Spurred on by their patriotic ideals, the Stuparich brothers enrolled under false names as volunteers in the First Regiment of the Granatieri di Sardegna or Sardinian Grenadiers (Bertacchini, 43), where they served with draftees from various regions of Italy, many of whom were bewildered by the Triestine brothers' decision to risk their lives in this way. The Grenadiers with whom Giani and Carlo served were deployed to the hills of the Carso near the small city of Monfalcone, and the siblings could often see Trieste from where the fighting against the Austrians raged. During their struggles in this inhospitable but sometimes oddly beautiful landscape, the Italian forces suffered tremendous losses. Stuparich has left an account of the two months he spent in these trying circumstances of trench warfare and sometimes hand-to-hand combat in a work based on diary entries made at the front. This brief book called, simply, *La Guerra del '15* ("The War of '15"), which was not published until 1931, is considered by many to be one of the most powerful and compelling accounts of this period in Italian military and civil history. In it we see for the first time the style that will become Stuparich's throughout his career: personal but reserved, unrhetorical but morally engaged, documentary but shot through with lyrical passages as well (Arosio, 165).

In addition to these harrowing pages about his participation in the war, Stuparich has left luminous descriptions of the happy years he enjoyed in Trieste and Istria before he went off to pursue university studies elsewhere. In these stories and essays, his warm relationship with his younger brother and the often blissful times they spent together at the seaside and other locations in this Adriatic peninsula are prominent. Later, both the Stuparich brothers were to be transparently fictionalized in Giani's novel of 1941, *Ritorneranno* ("They Will Come Back"). In this semi-fictional account of the author's military experiences, two brothers fight side by side in the war against Austria just as Giani and Carlo did, but only one of them returns from the hostilities. At the novel's conclusion this surviving brother is gravely injured physically though spiritually reborn in a Christian sense. While Carlo Stuparich did die in the war (he committed suicide rather than be taken prisoner while wounded and surrounded by Austrians who would have hanged him as a traitor), Giani was captured just as Carlo was afraid would happen to him. The older brother, however, was able to conceal his identity during his confinement in Hungary and elsewhere and then return to Trieste at the war's end. In 1922 he was awarded a Gold Medal of Valor from the Italian government for his military activities. Thinking later about the years when he was a prisoner of war, Stuparich recalled how "every night for two years I would hear ring out, in the silences when I was suddenly awakened, the measured footsteps of the Austrian guard who was coming to get me and take me to the gallows" (*Trieste nei miei ricordi* [hereafter TNMR], 110). It was during this period of forced detention that Stuparich began to sketch out an early version of some of the events that would later be central to *One Year of School.*

The Stuparich (originally Stuparovich) family's most immediate origins were in Lussino, a largely Italian-speaking fishing and maritime village in Istria. This heart-shaped peninsula lies south of Trieste and east of Venice in the Adriatic Sea, and figures in many of Stuparich's most personal writings. It is particularly important in *The Island*, which is set in Lussino and the surrounding area, though in the text the town is never mentioned by name. During the days of Giani Stuparich's childhood and youth, Istria, which had originally been settled by

Italians from Venice and elsewhere in Italy together with others from many places, was part of the Austrian Empire. After the First World War, it became Italian, then Yugoslavian, and is now a part of the Republic of Croatia. Stuparich's mother, a converted Catholic, came from a Jewish family in the Austrian interior. Other Stuparich family members had included ships' captains and others active in maritime affairs as well as a noted opera singer whose statue in the village is mentioned in the novella. There is a passage in one of Stuparich's first books, *Colloqui con mio fratello* ("Conversations With My Brother") of 1925 in which the author speaks with pride (and in the flowery D'Annunzian manner popular at the time) of his family's seafaring accomplishments over the generations. In it he warmly evokes "the paternal bloodline which flowed to our father from barbarians but was like a surge of energy and generosity, together with the salt air and adventures in far-off seas: ancient pirates who taught dare-devil navigation in Rome and Venice succeeded by shipowners who lofted their thriving sails throughout distant aquatic byways: grandfather returning to rocky Lussino after lengthy meanderings, back to a Homeric land fragrant with seaweed and with thyme, with salt-covered olive trees and cicadas!" [*Colloqui con mio fratello*, 69.] Given this passionate attachment to the land where his family had lived for centuries, Istria's change of sovereignty was a painful wrench for Stuparich as it was for many other Italian-speaking inhabitants of the region. In a number of his essays about the area, Stuparich refers bitterly to what seem to him these unjust forced transfers of nationality and, in many cases, of populations as well.

During the Fascist era, with Istria still Italian, Stuparich was hailed as a patriotic hero in accolades that often made him uncomfortable. His relationship with Fascism was a complicated one. On the one hand, he was a war hero respected as such by the strongly pro-military government in Rome. On the other hand, Stuparich never made a secret of his ethical and political reservations regarding Mussolini's regime. And then, frighteningly, after having endured imprisonment under the Austrians in the First World War, he was imprisoned again during the Nazi occupation of Trieste. This time he was not alone but accompanied by his mother and wife, both of whom were deemed Jewish by the authorities. Although all three of the Stuparichs were in danger of being dispatched to an extermination camp like that of San Sabba in Trieste where they were temporarily confined, in the end, they were released, thanks to the intervention of the Bishop of Trieste together with the city's Prefect.

In his final years, Stuparich became a kind of cultural patriarch in his home city. The Istrian native, poet, and Svevo biographer Lina Galli has described how after the war, the writer was "put onto an altar" by his fellow Triestini. "Trieste," she writes, "wanted him to serve as a figurehead who summed up in his person all of its highest ideals," even though it was an uncomfortable burden "for a man who was an artist to have been transformed into a symbol" (Galli, 61).

Both *One Year of School* and *The Island*, then, were composed by a writer surrounded by the ghosts of his brother, his best friend, and many of his classmates, all of them killed in the war. Both stories, however, are imagined taking place before the war and the life-changing events that conflict brought to young men like the son in *The Island* and the students in *One Year of School*. From the very beginning, readers of these stories recognized this. Their awareness that the events described in these tales had taken place before what was for many an apocalyptic period in their lives added an additional note of powerful pathos to the texts' receptions. This pathos was to become even more explicit in the film of *One Year of School* made by Franco Giraldi in 1977. In Giraldi's retelling of Stuparich's story, the action is moved forward from the academic year 1909-10 to that of 1913-14, that is to just before Italy's intervention into the conflict and the departures immediately after their graduation of the young men on which the story focusses. The high spirits, disappointments, and passions that this group of individuals on the brink of adult life experience in its pages were for many the last they were to know before the war closed in on them.

Throughout his career, Stuparich often chose adolescents or young adults as the principal characters of his fiction. At the same time, he also wrote about people at the ends of their lives. This was the case for *La morte di Antonio Livesay* ("The Death of Antonio Livesay") of 1929 and for *La vedova* ("The Widow") of that same year. Such writings often involved descriptions of the vulnerable, whether young, still inexperienced men, lone women, or an older man like Antonio Livesay, as he faces the final moments of an unexceptionable but to him still precious life. The two stories presented in this volume focus on post-adolescent men (and, in *One Year of School*, a charismatic young woman) who are struggling with the distressing aspects of an existence they are just beginning to confront. In *One Year of School* these issues, which include the recognition of the precarious nature of life and its ultimate finitude, are wrestled with collectively by an entire class of students, while in *The Island* they are dealt with by the slightly older and painfully solitary central character of the tale. The rhythm or lyrical tone of the two stories is quite different as well. That of the pulsating *One Year of School* might be described as *andante agitato*, while that of *The Island* is instead a pensive *lento elegiaco*.

Both these stories were written and published during Fascism: *One Year of School* in 1929, and *The Island* in 1941. During the years from 1922 to 1943, when Mussolini's authoritarian government dominated political and cultural life in Italy, much of the fiction produced in that country was characterized by a turning away—in part perforce, given the prevailing political atmosphere—from reflections on politics and the ethical choices involved in political action (themes that had often been central in earlier writings and were to become extremely important in the fiction of political commitment after the war) to concentrate instead on intimate and often autobiographical revocations of childhood or adolescence. Distinguished examples of such work include novels like Alberto Moravia's *Gli indifferenti* (*The Time of Indifference*), which was published the same year as *One Year of School,* and Romano Bilenchi's *Conservatorio di Santa Teresa* (*The Conservatory of Santa Teresa*), which came out in 1940, that is, at about the same time as *The Island.*

One Year of School was one of the first of Stuparich's stories to see print. In his volume of autobiographical essays, he describes the moment of inspiration that led to its composition. In 1921, after his return from the war, Stuparich accepted a teaching position at the Dante Alighieri high school in Trieste, an institution where he had previously been a student. It is at the Dante Alighieri that much of the action of *One Year of School* is set. In the essay in *Trieste nei miei ricordi*, Stuparich describes a personal epiphany that he experienced during a visit to the deserted school during summer vacation. He characterizes this moment as a kind of "enchantment ... that provided a radiant opening into a world that up to then had been obscurely and chaotically chafing within me" (TNMR, 124). It was this instant of enchantment, he claims, that led to the writing of the novella.

While the magical moment of inspiration in the front hallway of the empty school that Stuparich describes here was no doubt something that gave the most immediate impetus to the composition of this text, recent research by Giulia Perosa and others has shown that Stuparich had been thinking about at least its central incident—that is, the eventually painful love affair between two of the students at the school—for many years, beginning while he was fighting in the Italian army. We also now know that he spent some of the time when he was a prisoner of war sketching out the story both mentally and on paper. There is also a letter from 1916, and thus even before his imprisonment, to Elody Oblath, Stuparich's future wife, in which he refers to recurrent and troubling dreams of a love affair of his own that is very similar to that between Giorgio and Edda in the novella (Sandrini, "Amore e giovinezza," 79-80). At the same time, while *One Year of School* has a precise autobiographical basis, its author has insisted that the story it tells is not merely a personal one. The book's narrative, he notes in his autobiographical essays, deals with youth in general and as such is "something that didn't just belong to me or to a limited number of people but is the property of everyone" (TNMR, 123). It should also be remembered that *One Year of School* was completed after Stuparich had been not just a student but then also a teacher at the Dante Alighieri for several years. His experiences in that more detached position at the school provide the narration with a double perspective: that of the students embroiled in their own, often burning, personal issues, and that of their professor observing them with affectionate irony that is perhaps somewhat nostalgic as well.

Other characters in the text are also based on real people, many of whom went on to become important members of the Triestine and Italian intellectual establishment. The model for Mitis, for example, was Ruggero Timeus, who later became a follower of the nationalist activist Enrico Corradini before also dying in the war. The character of Edda Marty, whose first name was perhaps a nod to Hedda Gabler in Ibsen's play by that name, was based on Maria Prebil, a classmate and romantic interest of Stuparich's during his school years. Like the character in the story, who was determined to study medicine at the university, Prebil went on, after graduation from the Dante Alighieri, to become a distinguished pediatrician (See also TNMR, 167).

It should also be noted that the suicide attempted by Pasini (and contemplated by Giorgio) in the novel had counterparts in the numerous suicides by young intellectuals and others in the Trieste of this period. These include that of Anna Pulitzer, who was at one time an adoring component of Scipio Slataper's female retinue, as was Elody Oblath, eventually, instead, Stuparich's wife. Of greater importance for the history of Italian culture was the suicide of the philosopher Carlo Michelstaedter from nearby Gorizia and a member of the same generation as Slataper, the Stuparichs, and Spaini. As Thomas Harrison has demonstrated in his study of Michelstaedter's generation in the Austrian empire, Michelstaedter's philosophical writings remain painfully emblematic of a tragic *Weltanschauung* shared by many of these individuals during the years before and after those described in *One Year of School*.

The Island was published in 1942, one year after *Ritorneranno*, the full-length novel that was Stuparich's commercially most successful work. Its author's exceptionally frank account of the war in that book, however, was attacked by critics faithful to the regime as contrary to Fascist ideals and therefore anti-Italian, especially since Stuparich was already suspect as half-Jewish. *The Island,* which came out shortly afterward and today is considered Stuparich's masterpiece, is in some ways a reprise of *La morte di Antonio Livesay* in that one of its major themes is, as Stuparich said about the earlier story, "the problem of the solitude of a man who knows he is about to die and the atmosphere of incommunicability that has built up inexorably between him and other people" (TNMR, 129). In this instance, however, the center of the narration is not the dying man himself, as was the case for the spiritually isolated Antonio Livesay, but the son who watches his father confront his final days with a mixture of defiance, terror, and compassion for the offspring he is about to leave but has never come to really know, except perhaps during these, the last days of his life.

The Island was written during a period when Stuparich was disconsolate over events in his country, with Fascism temporarily triumphant, and unhappy in his personal life as well (TNMR, 187). He was led to write it, he has said, in response to a powerful image that had pursued him for a decade, especially in his dreams. This image is evoked in a striking episode toward the story's conclusion when the two main characters walk together along a country road in the noon-day heat past shuttered villas and menacing agave trees. Stuparich had walked along such a road on his way to Cigale on a sweltering day ten years earlier with his own father who was also about to die from cancer [TNMR, 201, ff.] Being able to write about his painful relations with someone the writer loved but had not been physically or emotionally close to for most of his existence helped him resolve his mixed feelings for his father and in this way marked an important turning point in his life. Partly for this reason, Stuparich was very satisfied with the story, which he completed quickly. *The Island* was the first of his books to be translated—in this case into German—and this too was a source of satisfaction for its author since this event marked a reconnection with the Germanophonic culture of Vienna after the terrible interval of the war. Although this is the first English translation of *The Island,* the work has also been translated into French, Croatian, Dutch, Spanish, Catalan, and Portuguese as well as German.

Works Cited

Arosio, Sandra. *Scrittori di frontiera. Scipio Slataper, Giani e Carlo Stuparich.* Milan: Guerini, 1996.

Bertacchini, Renato. *Stuparich.* Florence: La Nuova Italia, 1968.

Galli, Lina. "Come ho visto Stuparich." *Pagine istriane,* XIII, 10 (December 1963): 61-65.

Harrison, Thomas J. *1910. The Emancipation of Dissonance.* Berkeley: University of California Press, 1998.

Perosa, Giulia. "Dall'esperienza al racconto: *Un anno di scuola* nelle carte inedite di Giani Stuparich." *Studi novecenteschi* XLV, 96 (2018): 277-296.

Sandrini, Giuseppe. "Amore e giovinezza nella Trieste asburgica," in Stuparich, *Un anno di scuola*, pp. 77-86.

Sandrini, Giuseppe. "Padre e figlio nell'azzurro dell'Adriatico," in Stuparich, *L'isola*, pp. 89-99.

Stuparich, Giani. *Colloqui con mio fratello.* Ed. Cesare De Michelis. Venice: Marsilio, 1985.

-----. *Guerra nel '15.* Ed. Giuseppe Sandrini. Macerata: Quidlibet, 2015.

-----. *L'isola.* Ed. Giuseppe Sandrini. Macerata: Quidlibet, 2019.

-----. *Racconti.* Ed. Cinzia Gallo. Rome: Aracne, 2015.

-----. *Ritorneranno.* Milan: Garzanti, 1991.

-----. *Trieste nei miei ricordi.* Milan: Garzanti, 1948.

-----. *Un anno di scuola.* Ed. Giuseppe Sandrini. Macerata: Quidlibet, 2017.

One Year of School

(1929)

The light of a hot, noisy September morning was pouring through the skylight into the deserted atrium. Outside, the pleasures of vacation with its amusements and dips in the ocean were still whipping about like holiday flags. From the second-floor loggia, snatches of laughing voices were echoing now and again against the columns and causing a din in the atrium.

A small group of returning students had gathered up there. Young men of an old-fashioned sort, they had occupied that atrium for seven years and moved about very much at their ease; but their actions were restrained by a vague sense of respect and apprehension. If someone raised his voice in excitement, the others immediately looked around with concern. He himself seemed startled. Every now and then, they would turn their attention to a doorway, over which a painted white disc announced in black letters that this was the Seniors' classroom. In just a few days, they were going to walk through that door, a thought that made them both nervous and proud. But they didn't gather there that morning to look at the door of their classroom, thus sacrificing a wonderful swim on a vacation day. Their curiosity had been piqued by something quite different. On the other side of that door, Edda Marty was grappling with the Latin test. Edda Marty was a very brave girl, the first to try for a place in that all-male school. To take an exam in eight subjects and be tested on five years of Greek and seven of Latin was no laughing matter.

Was she going to make it? Was she going to become a classmate? Those young men had heard amazing things about her intelligence, but only one of them was fairly well acquainted with her. The others had seen her for the first time that morning when she walked down the corridor accompanied by two professors and went into the classroom. None of them knew how to deal with what they'd seen: two large and cheerful friendly eyes that had made all their hearts beat faster.

Marzi, a big beanpole who pronounced his r's as if they were l's, was the only one in the group who claimed to be well acquainted with her. But he wouldn't say either how or where he'd come to know her, even as he was bearing the brunt of their questions. Some wanted to know how old she was; some wanted to know who her family was, what school she'd gone to, with whom she'd studied; others, bolder, wanted to know what she was like physically and morally; and Mitis, a brooding face with malicious eyes and a cynical mouth, asked Marzi if he really knew her *"intus et in cute,"* inside out. At this, Marzi blushed angrily and would say nothing more while the others burst out laughing and then hushed up, doubled over with repressed laughter.

A little before noon, Edda Marty emerged from the classroom. Her face was a bit flushed and she was clutching her straw hat with bunches of cherries on each side. The boys swarmed all around her. Marzi, caught off guard, tried to wedge in to make proper introductions, but nobody paid any attention to him.

"How did it go?"

"Was it hard?"

"What was it like?"

Then, looking at them in turn, she answered confidently, little nods of her head accompanying the no-nonsense words that whistled a bit through her teeth. Finally, she dismissed them all with a "Good-by, I have to go," and ran down the stairs; Marzi raced after her while the others just looked at each other.

"Quite a character," said Neranz, all red in the face.

"She's treating us like friends already," observed Vitelli in some amazement.

"Oh, come on, you'd rather she be more formal?" Pasini retorted ironically.

"Anyhow," offered Mitis who'd grown serious and was twisting his mouth into an even more cynical sneer, "all I can say is that if that little girl gets into our class, she's going to be the ruination of us all."

*****

According to Edda, everything had gone wrong; at the end of each exam, she had wanted to give up, thinking she had failed. Instead, she passed with flying colors. "She always predicts disaster just so her success will be a real stunner," sniped Mitis.

Edda was a pessimist, like all fearless intellects. In life, she threw herself headlong into difficulties, never quite sure how she would get out of them.

When she was fifteen, she'd run off to Vienna to her be with her sister who was studying at the university. The sister was so much older and luckier than she was. Why hadn't she been born eight years earlier like Hedwig? Why didn't she live in a real city like Vienna, where women could smoke, go to cafés, come home late at night, and be treated as equals by men—even get into arguments with them? She still remembered the first years that she'd spent in Vienna—how old was she then? a little over seven—when from the window, she would see Hedwig coming home from school accompanied by a noisy group of students. Sometimes, just outside the door, she would see her squabbling with the men and pulling their caps off; and when they pulled hers off, she would think, how pretty Hedwig was with her short hair flying and her face all heated from the struggle! She had waited impatiently for the years to go by so that she could act that way too. But then fate stepped in with an unhappy decision from her parents—to move to Trieste and take her with them. It was a big commercial port, they said; but in reality, it was a small provincial city. And life there was completely different. The girls at her elementary school looked at her as if she were some exotic animal. They were spineless, their bravery consisting only of malicious whispers about other people; they shrank into their little skirts when she would propose some naughty prank on the teachers or a dangerous but exciting invasion of the boys' wing of the school. She learned the language right away, and within two years, she spoke like a native. In fact, she liked the language the Italians spoke and even preferred to speak Italian at home with her father, who was just able to stumble his way through it. But she liked the sea even more. She took a walk along the pier every day, went on boat trips and out for swims—swims in every season. But even when swimming, she had to put up with the whole gamut of small-minded provincialism. No, she'd never adjust to the simple, middle-brow customs of the people there.

They enrolled her in a high school for girls. She couldn't stand it. The older she got, the more she felt that that was no life for her. Whenever she met a boy her same age, she would be jealous and feel an uncontrollable urge to put on pants herself and cut her hair short. At least he could wander the streets by himself, break into a run if he felt like it, jump over the pillars at the pier and, when out swimming, do the craziest gyrations and make the most imaginative and daredevil dives he wanted to. When her sister came at holiday time to spend a week with the family, she complained, grumbling and distressed, about her lack of freedom and the stifling of her very essence. Hedwig would give her a pat, let her blow off steam, and try to calm her down. "When you're grown up, you'll be mistress of your own destiny," she would tell her and give her books to read that she devoured at night. Certainly, if her sister hadn't been there every now and again…

But one year her sister didn't come, so Edda, unable to bear it any longer, ran off to Vienna. She found Hedwig in her room, wrapped in a cloud of smoke, with her feet entwined with those of a young man. He was smoking too and was slumped like her into the opposite corner of the sofa. He had a glistening, shaved head and his face, which was even shinier, had two penetrating eyes behind two circular lenses. Standing perplexed at the doorway, she took an instant dislike to that man; she was about to hurl her suitcase at him, except that she was too intimidated by his yolk yellow shoes all tangled together with Hedwig's pointed black pumps. Hedwig, motionless, made it clear how surprised she was and showed a flash of annoyance in her glance, but only for an instant. "Come here, little one, my sweet," she called out with her caressing voice and beautiful, serene smile, "What a nice surprise! How are you?" And Edda, forgetting all about the intruder, rushed to her sister's arms and broke into relieved tears and laughter.

"Let me introduce my friend, Dr. Wieselberg," Hedwig replied.

The smoke was okay, the friend Dr. Wieselberg was okay, but those four entwined shoes weren't so okay with Edda, who was finding her trip to Vienna more disillusioning than pleasant.

Even so, she kept her focus on liberating herself from what she called the insular environment of women. As a first step, two years later, she decided to get ready to take the admission exam for the senior year at a boy's classical high school that she would use to pave her way to the university. The regulation was a recent one; all the other girls were too afraid to take a chance, but she was going to take the exam. And that's just what she did.

*****

The first days of class were like a musical instrument with one extra string: try as you might, you just couldn't make it play in tune. In past years those twenty young men, who knew each other by physical contact the same way ants do, would be delighted to return to academic life. After a few hours, the parentheses of vacation would close as if by magic. The grinds would reunite, as would the gangs of slackers. Even on the first day, or the second day at the latest, a general hubbub would reignite their camaraderie until the teacher, who had come in because of the racket, had no recourse other than a furious pedagogic outburst at the class, which at that point would pretend to have settled down into a pious silence. Once the teacher left, after several exchanges of knowing looks, the hullabaloo would start again. The teacher would return, furious, the door would slam, and, as punishment, the lesson would start a few minutes before the first bell. Almost every year, the same story: that was the downbeat, and afterwards, once the tempo had been established, for better or worse, the orchestra would continue to play without a maestro.

But that year it wasn't like that. No hubbub. Everybody felt they were hitting false notes. Each of them was struggling to recognize his former classmates in his fellow students, making a great show of being indifferent and nonchalant; but their uneasiness was actually quite apparent. The only person really at ease was the newcomer. Edda Marty talked animatedly with everyone; she walked around among her new classmates as if she'd known them for years, and she worked a transformation on them all. Saletti, from the silent loner he'd been up to then, became a brash conversationalist who was always one of the most prominent in the circle around her; Turez, instead of shouting out witty remarks from his desk in the back and making the entire class laugh, now usually sported a grim and melancholy scowl. For Mitis, Edda's arrival had triggered an endless burst of mental fireworks; he had never been so imaginative and colorful in inventing quips, paradoxes, double meanings; some of these were sharp and well-turned, but other times they were so heavy-handed and crude as to be downright dirty. Not only did Edda not seem offended by them, she listened to him with a smile and an air of superiority. Goading and sneering, they raised a ruckus everywhere, rascals and naughty fellows for whom "the woman" who'd been plunked down there in their midst had turned out to have given their precocious depravity an unexpected boost.

That was exactly why Antero had broken away from Mitis and Pasini. There had always been an understanding among them, right from their very first years; as they grew up, it developed into friendship. They got along well together: Antero's aristocratic reserve complementing Mitis's gruff, plebeian frankness and Pasini's loquacious good heartedness.

All three were students who didn't limit their intellectual life to the schoolroom. After school they would meet up for long and freewheeling discussions about literature. They didn't agree about the three poets of the day: Mitis was a die-hard Carduccian; Antero, a passionate Leopardian; and Pasini put D'Annunzio above the other two. When their spirits had grown too heated and their words began to sting, Mitis would suddenly start to recite Carducci's "Saluto italico," the verses of "Salute to Italy" whistling through his full lips and between his wide-spaced teeth as if flung out by a rabid passion that burned like a red flame in his tiny eyes. Antero and Pasini would tremble and fall silent; and when he was done, they would cry, "Yes, magnificent!" Because for them, far beyond any kind of aesthetic consideration, stood a love for the fatherland; the return of Trieste to Italy was their life's ambition. They were the ones who organized the irredentist rallies in class, who wrote a newsletter in which every word was a pledge to succeed in life in the name of Italy, and in which even their patriotic grandiloquence seemed spontaneous.

But Edda Marty had suddenly come between the three friends. Antero's interactions with her made him more polite; now he found his noisy, vulgar companions hard to bear. For Mitis, on the other hand, it was just the opposite; cynical as he was, he believed that women needed to be treated in the bluntest and crudest way possible. Pasini did not hold back; he didn't use the crude approach, but he did laugh at it with his broad mouth and his handsome black eyes, and, deep down, he was on Mitis' side.

Antero was sorry to have broken so completely with his classmates, but he preferred to stay on the sidelines and be by himself. And while everybody else used the familiar "tu" with Edda, he continued to address her with the formal "lei.

The first time that Antero and Edda found themselves alone outside of school, it was because of a mathematics problem. Although she was good at math, she hadn't been able to solve it.

"How did you solve that problem for tomorrow?" she asked him.

Blushing, Antero searched for words. "No, sorry to say I haven't solved it yet because I'm afraid I always do my homework at the last minute. But I'll try to come up with a solution right after lunch, and then, if you think …"

"Fine, I'm really curious to see what you can do with it."

They agreed to meet at five o'clock at the entrance to the Montuzza tunnel.

At three, with the problem solved and recopied, he was already on his way. He walked along the pier all the way to Sant' Andrea, retraced his steps down the Via San Michele, and then climbed up to San Giusto; from there he came back down, went through the tunnel and at four-thirty was at its entrance. After a bit, he saw Edda coming down the steps; it was a quarter to five. He was rather pleased and a bit excited at her punctuality.

They shook hands. She was quite red in the face. The corners of Antero's mouth were trembling.

"Already here? Did you solve the problem?" she asked, using the informal "tu."

Antero put his hand in his pocket to get the sheet with the problem; he unfolded it and handed it to her, feeling tongue-tied the whole time as he thought about that "tu." Why was she suddenly saying "tu" to him? Was it the customary "tu" that she used with all her classmates, forgetting that Antero preferred the "lei" form? Was it a special "tu"? A "tu" of friendship? A "tu" she was saving just for him?

"Oh, there it is! Of course, it was really easy; all you needed to do was introduce another unknown! Bravo!"

This time they looked each other in the face. Her pupils had a sunny glow about them, and certain emotions were playing across her mouth like hazy shadows on the grass. Antero was foundering in all that light. For a moment he had the feeling that it might have been better not even to exist because it hurt too much; he looked over at her almost as if begging her to put him out of his misery. Edda Marty batted her eyelids as if to create some distance between herself and that look. Her eyes now more measured, flickering with lovely golden specks, blushing. With her voice a bit whispery, she asked him if he would like to go for a walk.

They climbed partway up the steps without talking; Antero was beside himself with happiness. Edda Marty was all alone with him; school and classmates were no longer part of the picture; he could talk to her without having to always worry about others being around, far away from the persistent clamor and the jokes he found so distasteful. He felt his heart was bursting with words, yet when he tried to open his mouth, he didn't know what to say. And she made no effort to break the ice; she seemed content just to walk beside him in silence. But soon a conversation did develop based on trivial everyday topics; their feelings caught up in glorious giddiness, it grew into a thorough and lively exchange of views about utterly silly things. Antero didn't even notice that using the "tu" had become natural for him as well. They were friends, participants in a jolly, unselfconscious friendship.

The next morning at school, it seemed only proper to go back to calling her "lei." Except now the situation between Antero and his friends had changed. It was no longer torture for Antero to see them clustered around Edda during the breaks, with their awkward gestures and their faces somewhere between idiotic and hilarious; actually, he took secret pleasure in contemplating the contrast between all that and their walk on the previous day. He was also heartened by the glances that Edda occasionally shot his way from the midst of the group as if to say, "I'm not really with them, I'm really with you." In fact, it seemed to him that the unpredictable charmer was just playing along with the others, all as a ploy to reveal her true feelings to him alone. So, although he was relishing it, even smiling inwardly, he felt sorry for his friends, especially Mitis, whom he saw as so sure of himself, sure of having conquered Edda with his transgressive behavior, proud of being superior to all of them in her regard. Although he did feel sorry for Mitis, a twinge of pain was also dampening his self-confidence.

After school, Antero and Edda's encounters became more frequent; they went on afternoon walks almost every day. Her gaiety sparkled; she would play unexpected, naughty pranks, and Antero would go along with her; Antero, usually so serious, had no qualms about chasing her down the middle of the street, leapfrogging over the little pillars on the piers, playing catch with her hat with the cherries, laughing so hard that his whole body would shake. When he could, he would sometimes try to strike off on streets that were less busy and go on out into the countryside, not so much because he was afraid of how people would look at them as he was of bumping into one of his pals.

By now, school for Antero was an arena in which he was competing to win a flash from Edda's eyes, to create an opportunity to go up to her alone, even for a minute, if only to set up their afternoon rendezvous. They were happy days that he spent in a perpetual state of intoxication. He would wake up early so he could get to school as soon as possible and be the first one there, already seated at his desk to welcome her with a look as soon as she came in; he would go back home filled with elation at their afternoon meeting. He enjoyed the walks as much as she did and, once he had taken her to the door of her house, he would keep on walking by himself until the evening began to fall, trying, though without success, to put some order into the tumult in his brain and heart. He would reach home just in time for dinner, go to bed immediately so that he could be alone and, in the quiet darkness, re-evoke her image and go over the intellectual positions they had taken, what they had talked about in the days gone by while at the same time imagining what the days still to come were going to be like.

*****

That afternoon, Edda Marty was irrepressible. They had climbed over hedges and walls and gates; they'd crossed through private flower gardens and vegetable patches, at the risk of getting a beating or having stones thrown at them by the farmers or bitten by their dogs. Nonetheless, except for having been shouted at a couple of times, everything had gone fine.

Antero was a little bit worried and short of breath. They were also late, so much so that he let her go by herself on up to her house in the hills. This was the first time Antero had arrived home with his family already at dinner. His mother was waiting for him and hadn't touched her food; she looked at him with a pained expression on her face. Blushing and confused, he made up an excuse and told a lie. Always on the alert when it came to her son, his mother had been aware for some time that there had been a change in him, but she couldn't manage to figure out what the reason for that was; seeing how upset he was, tears welled in her eyes and a huge sadness came over her.

Edda Marty, on the other hand, made it a point never to tell her parents anything. When she got home that evening, she too found dinner ready. Her father was reading, her mother in the kitchen.

"I don't feel like eating tonight," she said, tossing her hat on the couch.

"But Edda, come on, sweetie, at least eat a little; how can you go without eating? Here, Edda, come here, my little one, you haven't even said hello to your dad."

Mr. Marty's hair and moustache were all white; his sharply contoured face was softened by two kind eyes. When he was with his daughter, he usually spoke Italian, but when he got upset, he would break into German. She was his paradise, a paradise that can only be dreamt of and never attained. Hedwig, the first child, didn't give a damn about him and always sided with her mother. He'd never been all that attached to her, and after she went off on her own, he had focused all his affection on Edda. He hoped that she was going to become something… even he wasn't sure exactly what; but at least he wanted her to be completely different from Hedwig, and to grow into a beautiful flower that he would cultivate tenderly. But to his great sorrow, and with a sense of pain that increased daily, he could see that Edda too was taking a path unlike the one he was dreaming of for her. This was her mother's doing, all the fault of that woman who had been his downfall. Who else could have bewitched him—a self-sufficient German—so much that he fell in love with her—a headstrong and standoffish Slav who was sickly to boot?

Edda did love him, but she paid no attention to him; and he had taken to not correcting her anymore. The day Edda said to him, "Listen, Dad, I want you to stop lending money," he had bowed his head and swallowed his tears: he'd done it all for her, for his dear little Edda, to provide her with a decent life, to give her a life of ease; and he didn't deserve such a slight. All right, he wouldn't lend anymore, if she didn't like it–and what harm was there anyway in loaning money to people who needed it? Usurer, usurer, the term was not fair! He'd economize more, put aside more from his salary because he wanted to leave a small nest egg to his naughty little Edda. That day Mr. Marty's kind eyes had filled with tears, and from that point on he didn't ask his daughter for anything more; he was satisfied just to watch her, to do all he could for her, to beg her for a hug or a greeting.

That evening, too, he wasn't up to asking her where she'd been; it hurt him that she hadn't even said hello and he was especially sorry that she didn't want to eat. But when Edda tossed her head and said "no," she was not to be argued with. She planted a kiss on her father's forehead and went up to her room. Then she threw open the shutters onto the cool evening.

Down below, the city was stretched out flat, its tiny lights clustered thickly and shining brightest where the land reached farthest into the sea. The dark water merged with the sky; it was only high up, above the reddish glow, that it was glistening with stars; fewer smaller lights dotted the dark mass of the hills. To the left below the house the single streetlamp on the road was giving off a feeble yellow glow. Edda took a cigarette from a locked drawer and went back to the window. She often spent part of the night smoking at the window. She didn't smoke in public; no one knew she smoked except her father who had seen her doing so but hadn't had the courage to say anything.

There, accompanied by her cigarette, her gaze lost in space, Edda Marty would fantasize. Up from who knows what depths, as the blood rushed to her head, came a horde of imaginary creatures, a jumble that she didn't try to put into any order; in fact, the more tangled the horde was, the better she liked it. She imagined herself riding on the reddish clouds of a sunset, leaping giddily from one creature to a perch on another; they had the weirdest bodies, part human and part animal, and their faces were all different, some twisted in pain, some smiling, some those of people she knew, others of strangers, and she delighted in patting or spanking this one or that.

All at once she felt dazed and her head began to spin; when she grabbed onto the windowsill, she could feel a sharp pain in her chest: a fit of coughing that she choked back so she wouldn't be discovered. It was the cold night air. Her blood was settling back down, but her head was heavy as a rock, and she felt even colder than the night was; only her cheeks retained a bit of warmth. It was at that point, even though her head was hurting, that she was able to concentrate:

that was when reality came into focus for her. In her imagination she could see in detail what Antero, Mitis, Pasini, Marzi, and all her other fellow students were doing; she could remember everything they had said, syllable by syllable, and the tone in which they said it too; and she could understand what they meant quite beyond what they were saying, since she could see in their eyes what lay buried deep within them; but she had nothing in common with those creatures; in fact, they scared her a little, making her want to say to them, "Hey, get away. Why are you crowding in on me like that? What have I ever done to you? What is it that you want?" And life as a whole so harsh, with its nastiness, its dangers, its prickly solitude—life as it now had begun to reveal itself to her, someone who'd always confronted it fearlessly—a life like that seemed a monstrous apparatus that should be shunned, or else be crushed; school, too, her studies, the scramble to get ahead without really being able to, spurred on only by the force of her will, where would all that take her? Without warning, her head stopped hurting and went back to taking control of the flow of her blood and, with it, her overheated fantasies.

A bit later she had another bout of coughing. "This cough of mine," she thought with her head pounding, "is just like Hedwig's; I heard it so many nights when Hedwig was lying awake in our room reading until dawn, and I would beg her, 'Hedwig, come on, turn off that light,' and she would say scornfully, 'Go to sleep, you're just a little girl.'"

"Hedwig! Where on earth is Hedwig?" She felt a pang in her heart; she could see her, as if she were really there, sick in a lonely bed, drained of energy, abandoned by everybody. "Hedwig, my dear sister, no, no I'm coming, I won't leave you, don't worry. Can't you hear the sound of my footsteps?"

Edda got herself under control. Below in the street there really was a sound of footsteps. At that hour? In the dim light of the streetlamp, the dark silhouette of a man with something shiny on his head was going by. Edda held her breath. A loud ring filled the silent house with alarming echoes. She rushed from her room and down the stairs to open the door: it was a deliveryman with a telegram. She snatched it from him and ran down the street to the streetlamp so she could read: "I'm not feeling very good. I'll be there on the morning train. Have someone come and meet me. Hedwig."

*****

Mitis, Pasini, and Momi had been waiting for Edda for half an hour at the corner of the Chiozza Porticos. The winter morning was bright blue and biting. The wind coming down from Monte Spaccato was strong and unrelenting. There would never be a better Sunday for the outing they'd been promising themselves: for sure there was ice at Percedol. But Edda still hadn't shown up. Could she have misunderstood? No, they'd repeated it several times: "Okay, then, at seven o'clock at the Chiozza Porticos." Maybe her sister was worse? Mitis was the most nervous, knocking together the ice skates strung together and hanging over his shoulder. His face was drawn and his eyes bloodshot. Pasini had twisted his broad mouth into a bitter smile, his white woolen pullover setting off his forever-hatless shock of jet-black hair and the black eyes in his wan face. The most relaxed was Momi, Momi the patient one, stubbornly close-mouthed. Devoted to Mitis, he followed after him like a dog.

"Three-quarters of an hour wasted, son of a ..." Mitis started swearing.

"There she is," said Pasini. In fact, it was Edda hurrying down the Via del Torrente; she was wearing a big white beret and a gray sweater; her ice skates gleamed at her side; she was leaning forward a bit as she walked, her stride a determinedly masculine one.

She was in a good mood. She shook everyone's hand, accompanying each greeting with a little nod of her head.

"I didn't sleep a wink last night because my sister was really sick; by dawn she was a bit better. What a gorgeous day! This outing is going to keep me awake. There's sure to be ice," she said, looking up toward the ridge of the Carso all spotted with green pines and white snow except for a few steeper stretches of gray rock.

Mitis and Pasini walked alongside her, Momi followed behind Mitis. Soon they were on the old road to Opicina. They climbed up it merrily.

"Mitis, you're in a bad mood today," said Edda with a provocative sideways glance.

"It's just that I'm stupid ..."

"We know that ..."

"No, I'm stupid to let myself think that women have hearts. They don't have hearts or brains, maybe they have something else ... but that's all they have."

Edda laughed and, turning to Pasini, said, "You know why he's always got it in for women? Because his girlfriend has to slap his hands when he comes on to her; don't you see how forward he is? He's always got his paws ready."

"You're just trying to provoke me. I've told you once and for all that girl-friends are like old traps that stink of dead mice and that I, on the other hand, prefer to sow some wild oats."

"Now you're just bragging. You told me once all about your blonde cutie!"

"Well, okay, that's all in the past, let's leave her out of this." Suddenly Mitis curled his lips spitefully as a trace of melancholy flickered across his brow. But he shook it off immediately.

"I've got it in for women and always will have because they're liars."

"Oh sure, that's all very well, and you never tell lies?"

"If I do, I tell them on purpose. But you women aren't even aware you're telling them. The devil has scrambled your brains."

"Oh, cut it out with that talk," interrupted Pasini, "between the climb that's making us huff and puff and the hammering of your punches and coun-terpunches …"

"Momi the Immaculate, what can you tell us about this friend of yours who's such a swine? I bet you're shocked. I for one have never understood how you can care anything about him." With that, Edda slowed her pace and slipped her arm beneath Momi's as he marched along calmly, bringing up the rear, his steps slow and regular.

Momi raised his head; he looked like he was swallowing some sort of li-quor dripping down from the sky. Then he bowed his head again and had nothing more to say.

"Momi gets it more than you think. He isn't surprised by anything," Pasini added.

"Momi," said Mitis through clenched teeth, "would be the only possible boyfriend for you."

"Why?"

"Just because he's never surprised by anything. And you could take that silly jerk Neranz for your husband."

"Did you know that Neranz has gotten really daring? Just yesterday he asked me if he could come to my house to ask my parents for my hand."

"So marry him, smarty. He's a millionaire."

"I don't know what kept me from bursting out laughing. Calmly as I could, I said, 'Neranz, old pal, we'll talk about it another time. Right now, I don't have a hand to spare.' And in fact, I had an umbrella in one hand and with the other I was holding my books by the strap so it would have been easy to smash them into that flat, wrinkly face of his; not to hurt him but just to see his ugly, gold-rimmed glasses fall off; he's always messing around with them just so they'll stick to that bell-shaped nose of his!"

Mitis sniggered. "You've put me back in a good mood with what you said about Neranz's nose! Whenever you're nasty on purpose at least, that's when I really like you."

Pasini flashed a wide mouthed grin and asked, "What ever happened to poor old Marzi? Did you treat him the same way you did Neranz?"

"Oh, Marzi; don't you say anything about him," said Edda. It wasn't clear from her tone whether she was really serious or just joking. "Marzi was my very first friend. We've known each other since we were kids and he taught me how to spin a top."

"Great, now he's the one who keeps spinning like a top. Although," added Mitis, turning to Pasini, "here's why you never see Marzi with Edda. There are too many competitors! And every one of them, so much the worse for him, knows how to pronounce an 'r' better than he does."

They all laughed, even Momi, who had kept a straight face about everything else he had been thinking.

"That's cruel," retorted Edda. "Marzi is ten times better looking than you are."

"Even if he were a hundred times handsomer, between him and me, you'd have to go for a third choice."

"Who, for example?"

"I don't know, Vitelli, Pasini, Antero …"

"That's three, not one."

"Right, though as far as a third one goes, you'll have to figure it out for yourself … it's a third choice to the infinite power. So pick as you might, you'll never figure out what to do."

Pasini didn't like the turn the conversation had taken; it was making him feel depressed. And when she heard Antero's name arrive from out of the blue, even Edda Marty had furrowed her brow.

"My, it's hot," she said stopping; she'd grown warm from the climb and her hair was sticking to her scalp. She took off her beret and was about to undo the top buttons of her sweater when a snowball hit her right in the chest. When it came apart it made her all white.

"Double-crosser!" she yelled at Mitis, turning on her defenses. There was some snow in a hollow below the edge of the road. The first one to notice it was Mitis, who in nothing flat had jumped aside, grabbed two fistfuls, and thrown a snowball.

The battle was on. It was Mitis against Edda and Pasini. Momi was staying to the side.

"Momi, you coward," yelled Mitis breathlessly. Momi seemed to be playing the mocking spectator, but, in fact, he was just waiting for the right moment; when he saw that Pasini and Edda, now certain of victory, were going after Mitis—either to drive him off or to bury him in the snow—he began to attack Edda in the back and head. Astonished, she was obliged to fight back. Taking advantage of this reinforcement, Mitis turned around to battle Pasini and drive him off; he whipped around, closing ranks with Edda from the other side. Momi and Mitis were right on top of her and threw her to the ground; in order to defend her, Pasini threw himself on top of the group and they all ended up in a tangle rolling in the snow, yelling and laughing.

"Enough, enough, you're blinding me" Mitis yelled because, as usual, once they were on the ground, it was all of them against just one.

They got up and brushed off the snow. Edda's eyelashes and hair were gleaming, but she was rather pretty all mussed, perspiring, and out of breath. Pasini was ready to fall to his knees in admiration, his pulse throbbing in his wrists. He was on the verge of tears but instead was forced to laugh and participate in that swirl of horseplay. Why, oh why couldn't he throw down his mask? Why hadn't he had the courage, a moment ago when they were rolling together in the snow, to grab her, press her against him, give her a kiss? Hadn't he sometimes caught a look from her encouraging him to do just that?

"We have to go," said Mitis, "if we don't, we won't be able to ice skate at all today."

They resumed their walk in silence for a long stretch, almost as if the snowball fight had worn them out. Pasini was still lost in unhappy thought. Yes, Antero was right when he told him that he couldn't put up with all that ruckus, that free-for-all of hangers-on around Edda. He'd done well to get out in time. Why didn't he ditch those two … intruders? Two intruders? No, Mitis wasn't an intruder, he was hopelessly in love with Edda. "If I commit suicide one day," he'd confessed, "don't feel sorry for me, life isn't worth anything." And if he kept on joking, it was out of despair; all you needed to do was look into his eyes. And Momi? Momi was lucky to be able to keep his feelings locked up inside, but even he must have been in love with that girl and maybe with the fiercest passion of all; he'd watched him a couple of times; when he thought no one was looking, his glance would settle on her with dreadful intensity. So there was no other way. Who was she going to choose? She ought to be forced to face the music once and for all.

Mitis had started making jokes again; his shrill voice cut through the air; it was so cold you could see his breath … which looked like the serpent in *Pinocchio*, according to Edda. But she wasn't reacting to his jokes anymore, and this irritated him even further.

At Opicina they ran into another group of schoolmates who joined them shouting enthusiastically, though Mitis and Pasini weren't keen on having this happen. But no sooner had she seen them than Edda rushed over to them and they got into a circle around her in a frenzied ring-around-the-rosy.

There was ice at Percedol but it was still too thin and Vitelli, showing off for Edda's sake, ventured out on it yelling "don't give way underneath me, don't give way underneath me." He nearly drowned and they had to fish him out with sticks. When he climbed back out, he looked just like an otter. He became the butt of all their jokes and the center of everyone's amusement for the rest of the outing. Some of them wanted to strip him nude; others wanted to shove him back in the snow as a homeopathic cure; still others wanted to dress him up in clothes borrowed from this or that member of the group. So he had plenty to do to defend himself. On the way back to Opicina, things got worse; Vitelli was as good a person as one could be and innocent as a child, but when Zottig set to tormenting him with brutal and vulgar jokes, he'd had all he could take and gave him a punch. Zottig, struck right in the face, turned pale, fell to his knees, and fainted; they had to carry him to the town pharmacy because the blow had broken his nose.

Along with Edda, Mitis, Pasini, and Momi seized the opportunity to break away from the group. They took the Scala Santa back down. The street was slippery. Edda had lost a heel and was leaning on Mitis's and Pasini's arms. Momi brought up the rear, as usual. Despite their efforts not to let it show, the tragi-grotesque consequences of their outing had depressed all four of them. And Mitis and Pasini had their hearts in their mouths when they could feel Edda's body brushing against now one of them, then the other. To take their minds off what each of them was thinking, they started to whistle a jaunty march tune.

*****

People were scandalized. This time she had really gone too far. That girl had gotten to the point where she had no respect for anyone, not even the dead. For days, in several families, especially those of Edda Marty's former schoolmates, people could talk of nothing but her poor sister's funeral. Even on an occasion like that, leaving her house to make a scene, to trample on every human and social norm! Why, had anyone ever seen a relative, a sister, walk behind a coffin dressed like that? With that little, mannish coat, ostentatiously white, with that big shaggy beret perched on her head as though she were in Siberia? Not her but her parents should be horsewhipped for allowing her to commit such a sacrilege. She had to have been either wicked or crazy because originality stretches only so far.

In point of fact, those were days when Edda Marty was suffering almost to the point of madness. From December to the end of March, from when her sister had arrived up to the day when she'd died, Edda was constantly at her side. Many nights she'd sat next to her bed and gone to school the next morning just the same, was even able to keep up with her homework and make believe she was happy with her schoolmates; even she wasn't sure how. She'd taken fewer walks with Antero—only one or two each week, just to be with him for a bit, because it made her feel better to be with him. He was so sensitive and calm that she found some relief in the things he said and the way he looked at her; he was maybe the only one who understood the sadness inside her. And if she had taken walks with other people, those were on days when Hedwig was feeling better and had urged her to go out and have some fun, get drunk on fresh air and silliness, since the burden of the pain, by now, was weighing down pretty heavily on her.

Edda would have given her life to save her sister. She had always loved her immensely. But it was only during those last few months that she had really come to know her. Hedwig, when she could talk, spoke only with her. She was calm, resigned to dying.

"Come over here, little one," she would call her and pat her head with a hand she could barely lift. "I'm dying but you have to think about yourself. Our enemy is lodged right here in our chests: we've inherited him from our poor mama; but you mustn't hold it against her; don't you see how terribly she's suffering? She knows … I saw her watching you sleep so innocently, pulling out her hair and sobbing, 'Poor Edda, you should never have been born; you're doomed to die just like the other one, just like everything I've given birth to.' She's the most unlucky and lonely woman I know. Love her. And take good care of yourself: live a healthy life out in the fresh air, build up your muscles; as soon as you can, take a long trip; get to know what your illness is and take control of it by pure will power; don't do what I did and go easy with it, allowing it to slowly take me over; so that now time has run out: now I don't even want to live anymore."

Edda wept in silence. She was still hoping her sister would recover.

"Hang on tight to your freedom to think and act the way you want to," she told her once again; "that's something precious; it's not easy to achieve. But you have to know how to use it—and to do it better than I did; all I did was waste my time. Don't trust the world. The other danger that lurks inside us is for us to be too easily fooled, to believe everything. Don't believe men if they haven't first given you good reason to. Don't trust their love, their superficial niceness; they're nice until they get what they want; men will be all over you because you're not just an ordinary woman; they'll come after you because you have an open mind; but if you give in, they'll wrestle your freedom away from you just as fast as they can."

"I don't believe in anything," Hedwig had told her the last time she was able to raise up on her pillow and say something. "I believed only in myself for as long as I had the strength to live; now I'm like a bow whose bowstring has gone slack. If God exists, He can't be anything except just bigger than other men and He isn't able to punish them for their foolish actions. And I don't want any priests or funeral rites or crucifixes; bury me in an unmarked grave."

Even so, they had insisted on the priest, funeral rites, a burial place in the cemetery. Edda objected to all this; she screamed, threatened; it was no use. She'd never seen her father and mother so firm and unyielding, supported by the other relatives who'd come for the occasion—that same father and mother who were too lazy to prevent her from going to wrack and ruin, unable to deal with her tomfoolery, had been ferocious when it came to the priest and the funeral, even though they knew that Hedwig's dying wish was not to have any of that.

And so, out of rage and desperation, she'd done some strange things. They'd gotten the priest, but she was careful not to let them put any funeral wreath, crucifix, or religious symbol on the body. They'd gotten the funeral, but she refused to dress in mourning clothes so that when she followed the casket, she would stand out among all the hypocrites following behind her.

After she had calmed down a bit later, she realized that she'd acted badly, that hers had been nothing more than a gesture that attracted even more attention to that grim hearse, pretentiously white, itself so ruefully different from the poor, humble, wasted body that it was carrying away. But in the end, she'd given in to her mother's tearful pleas and, though with Hedwig's words echoing in her head, had put on a simple black wool dress.

*****

She hadn't been to school for six days. She felt completely numb and spent her mornings and afternoons in the garden. Terraced, a bit unkempt, it lay on a hill overlooking the city. She would go down to the furthest level, which was narrow with a low wall at the end. In the corner next to the garden's big lateral wall, she would sit on a long, rough-hewn beam that served as a bench. A little arbor thick with vines sheltered her from the sun. In there, it was as if she were separated from the world: only the muffled sounds of the city could be heard and, every now and again, more clearly, the squeals of the tram and the striking of the clock in the piazza below. Beyond the low wall, across the open space, her gaze would follow the sky, sometimes pausing on the hill directly in front. It was strewn with little houses that seemed spots of color rather than places where human beings lived. She would bring along Ali, the dog that Hedwig had loved so much. Ali had become her friend; he would lie down at her feet; and both of them would stay there for hours scarcely moving.

At sunset that day, the clouds in the east were fluffy and pink.

It had been the first truly warm day even though it was already April; but spring had arrived late. Sitting in her usual place, Edda was petting Ali. For the first time in those last six days, her spirits felt a bit lighter.

"Edda, Edda." She heard her mother's voice calling from the house. She was astonished by that voice and that name; she didn't even remember that her name was Edda. And what could her mother want?

She went running. No sooner had she reached the entrance to the garden, a bit out of breath, than she spotted Antero in the hallway. She felt as if a fountain inside her had suddenly been unclogged and the spray it made filled her with happiness.

"Antero, come here, come here," she yelled.

But Antero was terribly uncertain. Hat in hand, he was looking all around; but he couldn't see her and didn't know which way to go. There was a dark pathway next to the stairs with the garden gate at its end: in the doorway against the light, there was Edda, slender in the shadows, waving her arm at him: "Over here, over here," she shouted. Finally, he saw her. When he came toward her, the dog began to growl. "Down, Ali."

"Come on. Let's go into the garden," she said, taking him by the hand and guiding him down the first steps.

Antero wasn't able to say a word. It had already taken a lot for him to go up to the house and ring the doorbell; several times he'd been on the verge of turning back, several times he had put out his hand and then let go of the bell pull; finally, as if in a dream, he'd rung it. He had taken Edda to the door of her house many times, but he'd never gone in.

Standing in front of him, Edda wasn't saying anything either and every so often would turn towards him smiling. That calmed him. He looked at her, dressed all in black with her arms half bare: the mannish rigidity of her body had disappeared, and her hair combed straight back and fastened above her neck looked less uncontrolled but by the same token seemed more subtly attractive. How those few days had changed her! He stared at her in the midst of her garden surrounded by plants that were still cold and leggy, just beginning to deck themselves out with buds. In that air, crystal clear in the first oblique light of the sunset, the garden where they were walking had something ethereal and fragile about it; it seemed that too bold a phrase or some awkward gesture would break the spell. But neither one of them was tempted to utter a word.

When they got to the bench, Edda sat down, and Ali immediately crouched at her feet. Antero stood for a moment looking at her; when he met her gaze, he could see a kind of plea in it for him to be straightforward, to be kind, since she was lowering her barriers, putting all her trust in how peaceful things were. At that, he sat down next to her. She lowered her head, cupping it in both hands. A deep note rang out; it wafted in the air, suffusing it with quivering vibrations; from the distant churches, wavering slowly, the tolling of the evening bells floated up and, like a golden sky above a gloomy mist, rose in its magnificence above the gossipy murmurs of the city.

Antero felt his heart swell with emotion. By nature melancholy and sentimental, he wished he could burst into tears and give in to that gentle, all embracing sadness. But he was reluctant to let himself go and start to sob while another, tighter knot was tightening within him alongside the more loosely tied one made by his melancholy. That girl so near him—the subtle scent of her body; the smell of her hair, her neck, and the nape of her bare neck, white and delicate, with soft, gleaming curls at the hairline, was turning the harmony of the evening's clarity topsy-turvy and arousing a stabbing torment in his heart and mind; his lips were trembling. If Edda had just raised her head for a moment, if she'd said something, he'd have been saved, she'd have been saved, everything would have returned to its natural order, everything would have been the way it had been before, the way it had been always. But Edda sat motionless with her face cupped in her palms, lost in an immense, luminous, pulsating void, but with her senses constantly taut and on guard: the waiting game she was playing was painful for her too. When she felt two hot lips on the nape of her neck, it was like a liberation. All the same, she didn't move; it was only when she felt Antero's arm go round her waist and pull her towards him that she raised her head, abandoning it on his shoulder and letting herself be kissed on the mouth.

*****

Kisses, kisses, kisses. By now all they could think of was kissing each other in a feverish thirst for kisses. They had moved the times for their walks to a later hour so that the dusk would make them less conspicuous. They hunted out isolated paths, alleyways at the edges of the city, the most hidden nooks and crannies; if the street that climbed up the hill was a walled one, they would stop at each turn, she leaning against the wall and he, having checked that no one was either coming up or going down, would give her a long kiss on the mouth. They didn't say very much—and never talked about their love, but chattered on about unimportant, remote matters. If they needed to see each other earlier in the day, they would meet at the end of some tramline at the city's edge. He would be waiting for her and then they would go out into the countryside.

Surrounded by rustic villas and small farms, a sunlit little road twisted up the San Vito hill onto the slope facing the shipyards and the Gulf of Muggia; halfway up was a gate that was always open. They would go through it and then walk a few steps further along a pathway. Once they had climbed over a hedge, they would find themselves in a small field. From there, unseen, they could take in the whole panorama of the sea and the hill before them sprinkled with houses as far as Punta Sottile. Leaning their shoulders against an old plow, they would spend long hours kissing and gazing at the view until the sun in front of them began to set.

Sometimes they would meet on a Sunday morning as well. "Tomorrow we'll just go for a walk," they would tell each other emphatically, as if saying "go for a walk" put kissing off limits. They needed to give their exhausting appetites a rest, a pause; and in fact the next day, filled with good intentions, they started off on what was just a walk, forcing themselves to reassume the carefree attitudes and bantering they engaged in when they were just two schoolmates who got on well and took pleasant walks together. But if something happened to turn their walk romantic—a word let drop with unusual force, sometimes just a simple exchange of glances—they would dive back into a state of burning excitement that lent their kisses a strong, sweet taste of blood and fury.

One cloudy morning, just beyond where the houses came to an end, they both had the same idea: to sit down on the grassy edge of the path. The countryside was completely quiet. It began to rain softly. He opened his umbrella and propped it against the sloping ground; underneath it, with the sides of their bodies on the warm earth and their arms folded as pillows under their heads, their lips met. The wholesome smell of the earth and the splattering of the raindrops on their improvised canopy began to make them feel intoxicated. The shower seemed to drench their burning thirst. When they got to their feet, they were completely soaked.

Another morning they met up on a craggy hillside dotted with a few low-growing junipers. They were nearly out of breath and sweaty from the climb; as they reached the top, they were greeted by a cold blast of the bora wind, which was just beginning to gather strength. The area was completely deserted; there was only a cabin at the top to defy the bora. It must have been a way station for some customs tax collector. They walked past: it was empty, abandoned. They looked at each other, desire blazing in their eyes. Inside there was barely room for them to sit next to each other on the narrow plank bench. He wrapped his arm around her waist and their mouths found each other. The wind whistled, howled, crashed; the cabin shook and creaked, its foundations groaning; it seemed that at any moment a more powerful gust might rip it from the earth. She was cold, and he locked her in his arms against his chest and kissed her neck, her hair, her forehead, and, once again, her mouth. If the wind had borne them up into the air and hurled them into the sea, still closed up inside there, they would have been delighted. They came out numb and chilled to the bone, and they rushed down the slope beneath the warm sun.

Such were the chance occasions that they took advantage of the moment they arose. But on certain days they were overcome by an obsession to kiss; and so they met just for that without considering how risky it was. Antero would show up unannounced at her house with the excuse of class notes or a book if it was her mother who answered the door. They would go down into the garden and sit beneath the arbor where they'd shared their first kiss; and they would nestle close together, suffering deliciously because they had to wait. They didn't dare kiss there in all that light since her mother's sharp eye could see them from beyond the foliage. But after a bit they would climb back up and, once they came to the shady little path beside the stairs, she would clasp him tight around the neck: it seemed that their mouths were never going to let go. When they reached the door, they were almost completely out of breath but said goodbye loudly so they'd be sure that they could be heard.

Antero was happy. And yet he was heavy hearted too. Except for the moments when they were kissing and he could forget all about himself, he was never at ease; dark thoughts would run through his mind. Just like that day, after their first kiss, when he had sensed that beneath that sweet happiness lay a bitter taste of death; that was why, after moments of exaltation, he would plunge down into dark and melancholy thoughts. He'd get home late every evening; by now, it had become a matter of habit; he gave up trying to make up excuses, and, seeing how much this hurt his mother, he became intractable and unresponsive, egotistically believing that the pain he was feeling was far worse than hers.

They had faded away for Antero, those wonderful days of happy walks when everything was clear and everything a source of carefree delight; the splendid days of going to school with his heart ready to receive and exchange their first glances of greeting, when the morning sun unhindered by clouds promised a brilliant day; when all he needed was just to see her, when walking beside her and laughing and joking without a care was the pinnacle of happiness—which sometimes spilled over into harmless wackiness and impetuous sprinting. Then at night there was the pleasure of remembering the day just gone by, and nothing else had any importance except his blissful longing to see the sun rise once again.

Now, morning at school was agony; those hours were torture; he would wait for her with a sense of anguish in the midst of all the things that kept them apart, and when their eyes would meet, it upset him for quite a while. Edda, however, was able to act the same way she always had with their friends and participate, at least apparently, in their foolishness; Antero didn't understand her; deep down, he found her frivolous, and that made him even more upset. He lived through those hours in fits and starts; he managed to calm down only when— with an immense effort—he was able to forget himself in class; at such times he strove to come up with the answer immediately and before the others did, making up for what he'd missed; once again he was the most brilliant student in the class; his translations from Greek and Latin were the most accurate and the most fluent. "The mainstay of the class," the Latin teacher would call him; though he didn't know that that mainstay was perilously attached, that sometimes all that was needed was for a "Miss Marty" to ring out in the classroom, and Antero would be unable to understand anything that happened afterwards.

And even when he could make sense of what was going on, it was with only the most unfeeling, superficial part of his brain. But good fortune continued to look after him.

It kept on protecting him even when the risk of being caught unprepared and distracted became quite serious and persistent. But at that point, due to an administrative rearrangement, the seniors were obliged to move into a smaller classroom on the ground floor. One result of this change was that Edda was now sitting directly in back of him.

Now he could feel her breath on his neck; when she bent forward, her hair brushed against his hair; her hand or arm would sometimes rest against his back. And then there were the little phrases whispered in his ear, to which he responded with notes. She replied with more notes that she would stick in his hair or put behind his ear or in the collar of his jacket or even, with terrible audacity, toss over onto his notebook or open book. An extraordinary correspondence about nothing at all but that was dense with meaning and emotions and reminiscences. And all this had to be kept hidden, carried out in such a way that no one noticed; so that Teuer, who was nearby, wouldn't be suspicious of anything. That effort consumed all of Antero's attention. He envied how she could juggle one thing with another, be ready to answer whenever she was called on. For Antero, however, class was just a blur, like fog before his eyes. Sometimes he'd have been in deep trouble if they'd called on him; he might have confused Greek with Latin, history with philosophy. He was often on the brink of such a disaster. Caught up suddenly by a "Let's hear what Antero has to say," he would get to his feet with no idea where in the world he was. Maybe it was habit, maybe it was courage born of desperation, but, most of all, it was good luck. All of a sudden, he would get his bearings like a carrier pigeon and go right on. Once he had answered, he didn't know how he'd done it or what he'd said. Still, his dreaminess didn't go unnoticed, especially by certain teachers; but they blamed it on overwork. "Don't wear yourself out, Antero," they would tell him in a fatherly way.

Edda Marty was walking on air. Except for certain rare moments when desire morphed into suffering for her too, knowing that she was loved by Antero provided her with a distinct sense of security; at school among her classmates, in her life among other people she circulated more easily than ever before; instead of losing sight of everything the way Antero did, her vision had become more acute; everything seemed simpler; she felt she could be more generous toward everyone. She started by straightening out Mitis; she'd noticed that he was straying from the beaten path and that it had been a mistake earlier for her to encourage this. Now she scolded him when he used dirty words and cut off his coarse banter; she'd managed to get him to talk seriously. Talking openly and straightforwardly, he ended up revealing the person he really was, quite a different individual beneath his mask of cynicism. One day Edda asked him why he'd broken up with his girlfriend, who still cared for him and continued to send him kind, heartfelt letters.

"Because I'm in love with somebody else," Mitis answered.

"Who might that be?" Edda Marty could tell right away how dangerous the question was that she had blurted out without thinking and she became flustered.

"I'm in love with you"; Mitis's voice came out as a shriek and his face went livid. Edda Marty managed to regain her composure.

"You mustn't be in love with me because I can't feel the same way about you. You have to go back to her. Let's shake on it and promise me you will."

Mitis lowered his head. He never did understand what happened in his heart at that moment. A whirlwind that has torn up a tree, its roots laid bare, upended on the ground … that was something like how he felt.

"No," he said slowly with an emphasis different from any before—the same way when, having escaped a deadly peril, you discover in a flash that you're a different person: "I'm not going to go back to her, but I'll write her and ask her to forgive me, I'll make things right. Thank you," and he grasped her hand tightly. "I appreciate it, you've been honest with me."

They'd left school walking side by side; he went on home alone. He didn't feel like eating and shut himself up in his room. For the next two hours he wept uncontrollably; then he brightened up. He had come to a decision: he was going to study and do things. Political activism was what he was born for; he'd provide Trieste with the bold vision and constructive energy that the city needed. He set right to work, undertaking a feverish week of research, quite beyond what he was doing in school and the homework that had to be done, but by now those were secondary matters, practical necessities; at this point school was completely behind him: in the library he read works of history, political tracts, all the newspaper and magazine articles that talked about Istria, Trieste, issues that had to do with the Adriatic region, irredentism; at home he boned up by reading Tacitus, Dante, Machiavelli.

It was a Saturday evening and he was at his worktable immersed in *The Prince*, when something startled him; raising his head, he saw Momi standing in front of him; he hadn't even heard him come in; Momi had such a disastrous look on his face that it frightened him.

"What's happened?" he cried out.

"He's killed himself," Momi stammered.

"Who? Who killed himself?" He was already sure who it was; he'd read it in Momi's silent face. Pasini, only Pasini could have been capable of killing himself; but he asked the question the same way a person who was clutching desperately at straws would ask it.

"Pasini shot himself in the chest with a revolver."

"Is he dead?"

"He's in the hospital."

Mitis couldn't rest until he got to his friend's bedside.

*****

"Yesterday Aldo shot himself in the chest. This morning he regained consciousness. He was raving and wanted to get out of bed to commit who knows what other craziness. He said your name several times. You have to come. His life is at stake. You're the only one who can make him want to keep on living. And if he can get back his will to live, the doctors hope they will be able to save him …"

Outwardly stony-faced, Edda was listening to Pasini's sister; inside, though, she felt like a curtain was coming down: all those things that had once seemed so clear-cut were now losing their contours and getting out of focus. Edda got dressed and followed her mechanically. The whole way, Hedwig's dying words kept ringing in her memory like a tormenting refrain: "Don't believe men if they haven't first given you good reason to"; but then other words of Hedwig's also came back to her that clashed with the first ones: "If you give in, they'll wrestle your freedom away from you." Edda, as if in a daze, didn't know what to think. Suddenly she knew what she had do: "I'm not going"; and in fact, she stopped in her tracks. But Pasini's sister, desperate, looked at her imploringly. And at this she kept on walking.

The endless, white corridors of the hospital made her imagine she was in the hallways of some convent into which she was being thrust—against her will and yearning painfully for life—by a relentless hand.

Pasini was lying there with his face marked by death. His black hair on the pillow looked like a crepe mourning veil framing the face of a corpse. When they drew closer to the bed, he opened his eyes. At the sight of Edda Marty, there was a flash in those eyes. Edda knew that what they were saying was, "If you're here, I'm going to live." She went over to the bed. Pasini's face trembled; he seemed to be waiting anxiously for something to ease his awful suffering. She leaned over and kissed his forehead. Just then, she heard Hedwig's voice saying, "If you give in, they'll wrestle your freedom away from you." His face relaxed as if a gentle calm had settled over it. Once they were outside the door, Pasini's sister threw her arms around Edda's neck, thanking her between her sobs and telling her that she was a saint.

*****

"Why did I have to bend down over him? Wasn't just being there enough?" Edda Marty kept asking herself that question all the way home. And when she got back to her garden, she collapsed on the seat beneath the arbor next to the low wall. Ali was at her knee, looking at her imploringly and wagging his tail, but she didn't respond with even a pat. The day was stifling, and large clouds were gathering over the hills of the Carso.

"Antero is coming over after lunch," she told herself dejectedly. But the thought of his name suddenly evoked his image. Antero. She wanted to brush the cloud from her eyes that was keeping her from seeing him. But she couldn't; in fact, that cloud grew denser and began to take the form of a pale head with a shock of black hair; it was Pasini's head. And then two eyes gleamed in that head, and a body took shape beneath it; and that body with that head was walking alongside her. The sun had set, there was nobody on the pier and they were walking along looking at the star of Venus shining brilliantly in the evening sky. Just like they'd done the day before. And Pasini was saying exactly the same thing he had said then: "Look, Edda, I'm in love with that star, but the star is cold and doesn't want me; and I'm all alone in the world; Mama really loved me, now she's dead; life doesn't have any meaning for me anymore." But she didn't answer; she was looking at Venus and smiling, though with a sudden urge, like the one she had the day before, to caress his hair. But he made her stop and his pallor grew more deathly and (this was new; this hadn't happened the previous day because then they'd said goodbye like good friends) he began to shout: "No, it's not enough, I want you to kiss me." At that, she ran off, heading toward the sea pursued by that pale head with all that black hair and the flaming eyes with no body beneath it. "Antero, Antero, save me," she wanted to scream but she couldn't; she could see him there in front of her, Antero, tall, serious, somber; he was stepping back away from her, putting more and more space between them while she was trying to throw herself into his arms. "I didn't kiss him, I didn't kiss him," she wanted to say, but she wasn't able to utter a sound.

A crash from up high startled her and shook her out of her hallucination. She realized it was almost dark. The sky had turned black and was roiled by the first clap of thunder. A second, then a third, and the rain came pouring down, driving, thrust sideways by the wind. Ali was wagging his tail and seemed to be waiting for his mistress to tell him he could get up; but Edda Marty, motionless, dressed as she was and with her hat still on, was inhaling the wind and damp cold and didn't seem to notice the water that was battering her face, running down her hair and neck, soaking into her bodice, and running in rivulets down her arms and hands.

"It's done; what's done is done," she thought quite clearly, "and now it's time to move forward. That boy must be saved. Hedwig used to say that of all my classmates that she knew, the nicest one was Pasini. 'That kid is OK,' she said the last time she saw him, 'though unlucky: deep down, he's a romantic.'"

"And Antero? Oh, how it hurt to have to give up all that happiness! But life is sacrifice. My sacrifice begins today."

She was soaking wet and shivering. "Poor Ali! Even you know how to sacrifice for your mistress' sake." She gave him a pat and got up; Ali gamboled about, not understanding why he'd had to put up with such a soaking before his mistress remembered he was there.

*****

The sky soon cleared and right after lunch Antero arrived. "Maybe no one will be home after lunch tomorrow; come then," she'd said to console him when they'd parted earlier than usual because she was going to go see Pasini; she didn't say anything about that, partly because it annoyed her to have to give explanations, but also because she didn't think it mattered if he knew or not. Antero had come in the hopes of spending a quiet afternoon all alone with her. And in fact, her mother had gone out. They were alone. They went down to the bench. Edda was trembling. "What's wrong? Are you cold?" he asked.

"No, no more; not today," she begged him, her face pale, twisting out of the arm that he'd wrapped around her waist to pull her against his chest.

Antero's arm fell motionless; he stiffened and bowed his head. He was an extremely proud person. It was out of pride that he addressed her so formally at school, out of pride that he didn't scold her for the silliness he so disliked when she let her classmates dupe her into putting up with their foolishness and jokes; out of pride that he never asked her what she had done during the day; he never asked for explanations of the reasons she alleged for cutting a walk short or postponing a date. And now it was his pride that was erecting an insurmountable barrier between them, just when what was needed was clear-headed thinking, bolstered by the unsullied friendship that had enabled them to look each other frankly in the eye and explain what was going on and be supportive and arrive at solutions together.

She pushed him away because she wanted to tell him everything unemotionally, knowing that she'd never be able to extricate herself from the abyss of kissing; and besides, she had to do it for honesty's sake because by now she belonged to another person. Yes, these were the careful words she'd prepared to say to him: "Pasini tried to kill himself because of me, and I wanted to—had to—save him. I can't be with you the way I was before. We'll keep on being friends. But I swear to you that you're the only one I've ever loved and still love now." But when she felt him go all rigid like that, she didn't know how to begin; she was proud, too, and that meant she couldn't insist on her sincerity to someone who secretly doubted it. And Antero did doubt her, he doubted her love; if only he'd said so! She'd have produced convincing arguments to persuade him he was wrong, and everything would have been straightened out.

Instead, after a moment of stiffness and silence, Antero got to his feet and stuck out his hand: "Goodbye," he said. It had been hard for him to say that "goodbye" without rancor.

"You're leaving? Why, Giorgio? Didn't you come over to be with me?" There was still time to salvage everything. Whatever response he might make— because you don't love me; because you're not the way you used to be; because I can't stand being with you if I can't kiss you—to all these things she'd have found a way to get him back, to take hold of the hand he'd held out to her and make him sit down beside her. He hesitated for a moment and perhaps was going to utter one of those responses; but then he shook his head and said, "I'm leaving because I have to study."

Edda was blindsided by such a lie, which lashed at her like a whip. She let go of his hand. She struggled to her feet and, peering at the ground as if she were skirting the edge of a chasm, she followed along behind him. Why resort to such an excuse? Why such an absurd lie? How could he pack into so few words so much calculated detachment, and so much determination to hurt and be hurt?

When they got to the dark pathway where their passion had so often caused them to pause and that for a long time they hadn't walked along without embracing, Antero grew confused; in a fury, he turned around and pressed her to his chest. She didn't resist a second time but let herself be kissed, responding with a kiss that to both of them seemed an eternity of bitterness that they savored like a paradise that was disappearing forever.

*****

An air of dark foreboding hung over the class that Monday. The news of Pasini's attempted suicide had already spread among the first to arrive. The eyes of everyone who entered the classroom were riveted on Pasini's and Edda's vacant seats, especially hers because everyone knew that he wouldn't be there, but it still wasn't clear about Edda. What was it the two of them had in common? Naturally, everyone was trying to figure out the motive for the suicide. Some were saying that Pasini had wanted to die because of the pain of the recent loss of his mother, though that was just a kindly rumor that Mitis was spreading and trying to render believable. But sitting behind Mitis was Saletti, who hadn't been taken in by it and was talking to his neighbors so stridently about the inexcusable recklessness with which "certain people" approach life that his unpleasant voice could be heard by everyone in class.

"Right," he said at a certain point, "it's all made up. If it had been about his mother, he'd have killed himself right after she died. No, Pasini was a hothead; I've always said so and he was just crazy enough to …"

He couldn't finish thanks to the powerful backhand slap that cracked across his cheek with such a smack that it caused everyone to stop talking. Mitis had turned back around, his hand ready to strike again; his face was in turmoil, his eyes bloodshot. There was no reaction from Saletti.

The mood in the classroom grew even more somber. Usually so devil-may-care, the students seemed completely transformed. It was that day when several of them realized that life has its own tragic seriousness, and school and all its trappings are meaningless in comparison. For a good while, the teachers found themselves facing a class that was distracted and inattentive, and they lost their patience; but they were completely mistaken about the reason for what was happening.

They had shaken their heads when they learned about Pasini's attempted suicide: but, for them, Pasini had always been a weak student, restless, nervous;

they didn't try to go beyond that, because "negative qualities" like those were more than sufficient to explain his "rash act."

Antero was among those who found out about the tragic event only after he got to class. He'd had a terrible night. Rushing away from Edda's house, he'd wandered about the city until dinnertime, not knowing where he was, beset by internal demons he was unable to control. Edda didn't love him, she'd never loved him, she'd let him kiss her as a lark, the same way she certainly let others kiss her, she hadn't been honest with him or with anyone, she was using her wiles to lure and torment them and the only thing that mattered to her was moving on, going from the arms of one person into those of another. That's why she always wanted to be surrounded by her classmates; that's why on this or that day she "couldn't": she had lots of obligations; that's why she had Mitis walk her home after school and why she chatted with Pasini and called Marzi over and would smile at Saletti. And he, he who'd been so suspicious at the start, he'd let himself get snared; he'd fallen for it the most stupidly of all; he'd sacrificed his dignity to her; who knows what fun they were making of him behind his back, all the others and her too; and he who thought he was above the others, who considered himself morally superior to them, was instead the most foolish and cut the poorest figure of all—in Edda's eyes as well.

Once home, every bite he'd swallowed at dinner had tasted like the bitter tears he was holding back. Afterwards, in his room, he'd thrown himself onto the bed, still fully clothed, and had sobbed desperately with his head in the pillow, biting it out of agitation and rage. To break free, free of her and of that passion. But how, how, if he was forced to see her every day, feel her breath behind him? If her eyes continued to overpower him and her lips kept on being so desirable? No, his willpower wasn't strong enough for such a long, protracted struggle; he was going to have to commit one single act that would end it all. He'd already had a foretaste of death—mournful and sweet—from the moment when he'd fallen for Edda. He was going to have to kill himself.

That's how he'd spent the night, among a thousand phantoms of death, and now he realized that while he was only fantasizing, someone else had already tried—and maybe succeeded—in taking his life. A brooding self-absorption was crushing him. Pasini, his friend, had beaten him to it. If Pasini were to die, that would cause a thorny barrier of remorse to be thrown up between Antero and Edda; if he got well, she'd be Pasini's. At this point, no one else mattered; that pale young man in the arms of death couldn't be turned down. Edda hadn't come to school so as to be at his bedside. Antero's gentle nature was overcome by feelings of almost barbaric jealousy. At one point, the lines from *Antigone* that the professor had asked him to recite seemed to be flashing at him blood-red from inside a thick fog. He wished he could have stopped and put an end to his suffering by telling the teacher, "I'm not feeling well!" It was true that he didn't feel well; but his pride, always vigilant, hadn't let him do that. When he'd finished reading and had to translate, he childishly uttered a silent prayer: "Oh, God, save me." After floundering desperately like a man gone overboard, he translated calmly and with touching gentleness the passage in which Antigone, on her way to death, turns to her fellow citizens: "See me, citizens of my fatherland, setting forth on this path for the last time, looking for the last time on the sunlight that I will see no more." He felt the same way he had as a little boy in his first years of school when, after a Sunday spent playing, he would realize late in the evening that he hadn't done any homework and there was nothing he could do about it. He'd go to sleep praying, "God, please don't let them call on me tomorrow, and I promise I'll say twenty paternosters tomorrow night." That had given him some relief.

When school was over, he didn't go right home but walked toward the pier with his books under his arm. In the already-hot May sun and to the intense pounding of the sea, he walked along, worn out after his sleepless night, and feeling dazed and sluggish. Confused thoughts were running through his head. He wouldn't go see Pasini; he didn't think he could; but maybe he'd find out everything from Mitis; though Mitis was wary of him; better to go find Momi, though Momi was keeping quiet about it. He decided to go to Mitis's after lunch. Or instead, what if he actually went to her house? He needed to get an explanation. No, not to her house, not yet. Looking at him the way she did, she'd have confused him and, as usual, he'd have seen only her mouth and everything would have ended in a long, bitter kiss, the way it had the day before.

But why hadn't she said anything yesterday? What a con artist she was! If only he could free himself of her! That's right, be free of her, free of all of them, not have anything more to do with Pasini or with anyone else. But then there was school, the recurring torture that made him stay close to her and to the others, his mind always tense and his heart in tatters. How could he quit school? The "duty" that every morsel of his upbringing and his mother's own exemplary life had planted within him—that "duty" was so deeply implanted he couldn't uproot it without killing the rest of his organism. Devastating though it might be, he had to follow the path that lay in front of him.

Faced with that insurmountable obstacle, he was in such anxiety that if wanting it so intensely had been sufficient to get what he was hoping for, he'd have fallen down dead right there at the edge of the dazzling sea.

What if he confessed everything to his mother? She was stern; but like that of a guardian angel, her compassion could always be counted on, and it was boundless. To lose himself in her embrace, the way he'd done so many times when he was a child and seek salvation there! Would that be weak? But he couldn't go on suffering like that forever.

Like a person who is mortally ill, he clung tight to this lone hope for a cure and he was feeling better when he went home.

*****

Edda had never felt so painfully powerless as a woman as she did in those hours after Antero's sudden departure. She was all alone in the house and had the whole garden to herself; to her it felt like a huge labyrinthine forest. Other times, and there had been many, she hadn't even noticed being alone; in fact, she was quite happy to be there by herself doing just as she pleased. Ali, her inseparable companion, wagging his tail beside her, had turned into a stranger; he made her feel frightened and almost disgusted. After shutting the door to the house, she'd gone back to her bench, but she couldn't be still; she went up to her room and the dog, left outside the door, began to whine. She threw herself face down on the floor like she always did in moments of great distress or extreme joy. Without realizing it, she was babbling words in German, fragments of a lullaby her father used to sing her when she was a baby. She couldn't turn her mind to anything rational. "Come, come and get me all of you," she murmured, "I'm just a poor, frightened child." She listened hard and imagined she actually heard someone coming up the steps. "Why won't you come back, Giorgio? You'll take me in your arms and carry me in the rain to that shack at the top of the hill and then from there you can take me anywhere you want; I won't stop you." She uttered lots of other disconnected, barely comprehensible phrases until she fell asleep with her head cradled on her elbow; meanwhile, outside, the day was dying in shades of purple and gold. She awoke in the dark and stood up shivering beneath the weight of a profound sadness. Tomorrow morning she'd go to school; her feelings of helplessness were getting the better of her, but she couldn't, she simply couldn't lose Antero like that.

The next day, at seven o'clock, Pasini's sister, all out of breath and sobbing, arrived to plead with her to come to the hospital. Aldo had spent a peaceful night; but as soon as the light of day came into his room, he'd started staring at the doorway; his breathing had become labored due to the long, pointless wait, and for two hours his fever had been rising and he was raving.

"I'm not coming," Edda replied calmly.

Pasini's sister stiffened; stony-faced, she made a tremendous effort to move her lips; when she was finally able to give voice to her words, they burst forth in a long-repressed stream: "You don't want to come? But don't you realize that you're the cause of everything? That you're the one who's killing him? That you're a cursed woman? Cursed, yes; and cursed the hour that you entered my brother's class. Cruel, yes cruel; what else to expect from a creature who has no sense of decorum who doesn't even take her sister's death seriously? Coward, nasty coward."

Pasini's gentle sister was no longer recognizable; her eyes were rolling, she seemed ready to fling herself at her. Edda, who had remained calm and kept a slight smile on her face during that whole awful fit of rage, had in fact felt her soul was being cleansed by the violent gush of those insults, and she made her stop.

"I'll come. Calm down. I'll be ready in just a moment."

Pasini's sister collapsed onto a chair, muttering as if in a daze, "You must forgive me… It's not true… I was carried away …"

They walked along the street together, just as they had the day before; they didn't exchange a word. Pasini was lying there semiconscious; Edda kissed his forehead and he gave her a pitiful smile of thanks. She sat for a long time next to his bed, holding his hand in both of hers. She wasn't thinking about anything, but she sensed that that was just how a mother would have stayed with her son—though Pasini didn't have a mother.

In fact, the idea that had popped into her head a half hour earlier when she'd changed her mind was this: "I'll go there and be a mother to Pasini." The thought had come to her spontaneously, unlike the hateful words that that poor woman, carried away by her rage, had vomited at her. If Pasini had had a mother instead of a sister, his mother wouldn't have spoken like that. Now, going back home from the hospital, she felt more at peace. Now she could even wait until tomorrow before seeing Antero again and calmly explaining everything. There was no need for dubious denials; they could keep right on loving each other; her feelings for Pasini were completely maternal.

*****

What a Tuesday morning! The storm during the night had cleared the atmosphere and the sky. The light and the cool air were filled with a healthy woodsy smell that the mountain wind was blowing down onto the city. Books under her arm, Edda walked down her street almost giddy. It didn't worry her a bit to think that she'd be subjected to her classmates' incredulous curiosity. Instead, she was cheered by the image of Antero; she could see the nape of his neck and his shoulders; she'd hide away behind them; the Latin teacher could drone on with his "Horace"; she would delicately insert a note between Antero's neck and his collar with these simple, sibylline words: "Watch out, Antero!" Who knows how he'd wrinkle his brow when he read that and how long he'd puzzle over it! But it was so easy to understand: "Watch out, Antero! Be careful not to lose me! If you love me, don't expect the impossible either from me or from yourself; let's just keep on loving each other!"

When she got to school and went into the already nearly full classroom, everyone fell silent; they weren't expecting her; all eyes, astonished and almost hostile, were riveted on her. There was a challenge in many of those looks. To cross the room head bowed and take her seat nervously in the back would have meant, "Excuse me, judge me as you will, go on and bombard me with your sarcasm." Edda understood that immediately; and so she stopped in the doorway, raised her head proudly, and ran her eyes over them as if she were wielding a scythe. She passed the test successfully; heads were lowered, and she went on by, smiling and saying hello left and right. Before she got to her seat, she stopped at Mitis's desk to ask what they'd translated in Latin the day before; she paused at Saletti's desk to return a notebook that he'd loaned her. She was in charge, as usual. The chatter started up again until the first bell rang.

Antero wasn't there. He hadn't come in the way Edda was anxiously expecting him to do at any moment; he hadn't sat down in front of her and screened her with his shoulders. She suddenly lost all her self-confidence. She could feel she was being sucked into that void that had begun to yawn in front of her. "He's not going to come," she said to herself disconsolately, her head lowered over her book, "and I don't have anything anymore, I'm lost." Rage and pain caused the blood to rush to her head. She managed to calm down only at the end of the hour. During the break, she put on such a pretense of exaggerated lightheartedness and happiness that Mitis was shaking his head, and Neranz had tears in his eyes from his delight at seeing her act like that. Not a word about Antero; she carefully avoided asking about him, but she pricked up her ears around all the knots of students to see if they were talking about him; nothing.

What had happened? Leaving school, she was tempted to go up to his house, but she'd never gone there, and had a holy horror of Antero's house. She was walking with Mitis, who was talking to her about Pasini, his voice quivering with emotion; but she wasn't listening; it upset her not to know how to find out what had become of Antero. The more she thought about it, the more it gave her heart a wrench. Maybe Antero had wanted to kill himself too and he was tearing himself to pieces in desperation. Before this, she had never even imagined that somebody might kill himself over her, but after what Pasini had done, the idea had become perfectly plausible. She was someone who brought bad luck to anyone who was close to her. On Sunday, after bolting from her house, maybe Antero had gone off and tried to do away with himself. She couldn't bear such a painful thought and so, cutting Mitis off in mid-sentence, asked brusquely: "Was Antero at school yesterday?" "Yes," Mitis answered in irritation. "Why do you ask?" "Because I needed to talk to him today," said Edda, relieved. "I'll write and ask him to come see me," she thought, "as long as he's not sick."

On her table at home she found a note from Antero's mother who wanted to talk to her that very day. The blood rushed to her face: that was the last thing she was expecting, and it upset her and made her gloomy and uncertain again. Besides not knowing what had happened to Antero, she was going to have to go, totally unprepared, to meet with his mother, a person who for some reason intimidated her. In the presence of all other women, Edda felt scornful and free because of how different she was from them. But she shuddered at the very idea of being with his mother. She'd seen her a few times, but her bearing and the worshipful words that Antero used in talking about his mother had always made her seem a creature from another, almost unattainable order of being.

She had no sense whatever of the room she was shown into; she didn't try to look around to see what it was like in Antero's house, where she was for the first time; she had only one thing on her mind: to get out of there as quickly as possible.

Antero's mother came in quietly. There was something unbending in her face and attitude. Edda didn't have the courage even to murmur a greeting. Besides, there was no need for them to say hello. She could tell right away that Antero's mother was her enemy. She lowered her head for a moment, all but overwhelmed by the beauty and haughtiness of the features and gestures of that still-young woman, whom she was seeing up close for the first time. But then she quickly raised her head and looked her in the eye. That direct, cold gaze was meant to say, "I'm not afraid of you," but then she became meeker and submissive and seemed to be imploring, "Be gentle with me."

Antero's mother began to speak; her voice was firm and resonant.

"Giorgio has gone away; I took him myself; I've found a way to resolve the situation. As far as school goes, I've had him excused because of nervous exhaustion; he'll come back a few weeks before exams, if he gets better," she said, emphasizing her final words.

"But he will get better," she added briskly. "And you, you get this into your head, from this day forward, you're to stop tormenting him."

Edda grew beet red; she gave a start and was about to burst out: "You can have your son! Who's doing anything to him?" but she held back, balling up her icy, trembling hands.

"You've hurt him enough; you can't even imagine how much you've hurt him …" And with this her voice suddenly faltered and tears glistened in her eyes.

"Do you realize that my children are my whole life? More than my life, really. It was for them that I sacrificed not only my youth, but all the opportunities I had to live my life according to my own wishes and ideas. I was once outgoing and instinctively kind, but I've grown cold and unpleasant with men just to defend my children—and I have defended them against everybody, even their father. My Giorgio, I've been there for him day and night all the times he was sick, including when he had the most serious and contagious kinds of illness; I didn't want anybody else to come near him. I made him into my own creation, considerate and moral, with pure and lofty aspirations. All I want is to see him in a good position in life, at ease and confident, more so than other men. But you … Oh no, let me have him…" her voice, wracked by sobs deep inside her, had grown imploring. "Let me have him. You don't know what it's like yet to be a mother; maybe you never will. You're surrounded by so many young men, all of them wanting you; you can pick and choose; but not him; he's mine, he still needs me. Yesterday, he cried on my shoulder like a little boy."

She had come over to Edda and had taken one of her hands in hers; she kissed her on the forehead as a flood of tears coursed down her cheeks.

"Promise me you won't try to make him stay in love with you, that you'll help me make him forget you. Do you promise?"

His mother's selfishness was unbearable, her request absurd. Edda couldn't say a word; she was overwhelmed, as if lost in some unnatural world;

she could no longer understand what it was her heart was telling her. She wanted
to disappear; to be able to break away from that nightmare, and she nodded in
agreement, disentangled her hand, and fled.

*****

Once in the open air, she felt faint. She quickly shook that feeling off and
began to reason calmly, the way a neurotic sometimes does, feeling a sudden
peaceful clarity of mind and spirit after a serious bout of nerves when everything
seemed a tragic mess.

Oh, how different Antero now appeared to her in comparison to the Antero she'd once known. He was entangled in a whole other life, a whole other
world she would never be able to understand or find a place in. Up to then, ever
since her sister had died, she'd permitted strange and almost contradictory de-
sires to capture her thoughts and fantasies; she'd often been slightly startled at
one of these: that of becoming Antero's wife. She'd always dismissed it because
she understood that it was a foolish option for her, alien to her character. But
only now did she sense the terrible danger that it contained for her. Yes, she
should be grateful that she'd had that encounter with Antero's mother, who'd
opened up her eyes. She had been on the brink of falling back, imperceptibly
but inevitably, into that bourgeois life from which she'd made such an effort to
wrench herself free, that arid, confining life that she hated. Maybe an hour earlier, if Antero had come to her house and said definitively, "Let's get married,"
she'd have said yes. But then, the dawning reality would have been awful: she'd
be weak once again, hating herself, lost forever. How could she have gotten to
the edge of such an abyss? How had she been able to lose sight of what she
wanted to do in life? What she wanted to do in life wasn't all that clear yet, but
she sensed that, however vague, it was more important than the scenarios—all
safe and soothing—that might be beguiling her at the moment. No, she had to
move on, persevere. She'd shattered the barriers that were blocking her quest for
liberty and had started down the road that led to it—why else had she insisted
on and succeeded in getting into that classical high school? Why was she studying—and was going to keep on studying at the university? Studying was the
price to be paid for that liberty; the professional fields that attracted her were the
domain of free and open interactions with men; she didn't want to be dominated;
she didn't want to answer to anyone but herself for what was her own life. But
now that she had been put to the test, she'd let herself be distracted by her new

companions, had acted almost like some drunken person in the midst of all those young men; she'd given in to the most ordinary and starry-eyed emotions—just like the women she detested. Love, for her, wasn't meant to be subjection; nor did she aspire to be the conqueror, the femme fatale, who, when cloaked in power and ascendency, is finally just as weak and servile; for her it was enough to never lose control of herself and always be able to disengage from the clutches of love when she wanted to. Deny that this was so … no; she understood only too well that denial would be a lie because she needed love, just as she needed to catch her breath in the shade after a long walk in the sun.

And Edda Marty understood a great many other truths just then, at nineteen years of age, in the midst of a crisis that was casting such an intense light on her whole being that, as never before or afterward, she could see deep down into her very essence.

*****

Pasini was getting better just as quickly as trees leaf out in a hot, early spring. The effect of Edda's daily presence on his health and spirits—even if she stayed only a few minutes—was miraculous. After two weeks in the hospital, he'd gone home, pale and thin; beneath his shock of black hair his face was all cheekbones, eyes, and mouth; he needed a cane to be able to walk; for hours he would sit, blissful, by the window. Beyond the roof tiles of the house across the street, he could see a strip of green hill and a piece of the sky; that's all he needed to become happily lost in thought. As it wafted in, the breeze enfolded him in its warm, sweet-smelling embrace. He had learned to love the fresh air, which soothed his spirit the same way that feeling Edda's hand did. When he asked Edda to sit close to him at the window, she would let him hold her hand, and he would take it tenderly in his two hands, feeling its blood quicken his own blood, which was listless and exhausted. Besides yielding her hand, if Edda were to have put her lips on his forehead the way she had the first times, his convalescence would have been like paradise. But even without that, how sweet it was to be alive. How could he have given up on life? It was because he had never really tasted its essence; now no misfortune he could encounter, no moment of sadness or desperation would be powerful enough to make him try to take his life.

But holding her hand and, looking fixedly at her face from up close, his desire to kiss Edda on the mouth kept mounting. And one day he finally pulled her toward him and kissed her lips. Immediately he felt ashamed; big tears rolled slowly down his cheeks; and then he spoke—about a happiness that was more than he deserved, about his total lack of comprehension that evening at the pier, about God's grace in having saved him.

Sobbing, he finally burst out, "Edda, my Edda," and put his head on her lap.

Edda patted his head. "I am fond of you," she told him, "don't let this make you sad, but I can't promise you anything, I can't leave you with the illusion that one day I'll be *yours,* in the way that a man calls a woman *mine.*

Pasini raised his wan face, asking in a broken voice, "So it was all a masquerade?"

"No," Edda replied drily; she had grown pale herself and her eyes were flashing. "I am fond of you, and you can go ahead and love me, but I beg you not to think of me like a fiancée or wife."

Pasini was determined to ask her what she meant, but she rose to her feet, kissed his hair and said, "There's nothing to explain; that's just the way it is. See you tomorrow." And she left him to himself.

How it hurt; and he didn't even have bandages around his chest that he could rip off so he could bleed to death! But enough of that; at this point he needed at all costs to keep on living. He smiled, sadly recalling the thoughts that used to come to him every morning at that very window about how good life was—and now, such a short time later, he could see it was irreparably bitter; as always, as always, except that between then and now there had been an inaccurate revolver shot aimed toward his heart.

That night he was fitful and didn't sleep, he repeated the words Edda had said a hundred times, but he couldn't make any sense of them; he didn't understand her, he'd never understood that woman; sometimes he hated her intensely. The following morning, he couldn't get out of bed; his fever had come back.

*****

But he got better quickly; Edda came punctually every afternoon and let him kiss her; some days he would take her on his knees and kiss her so frantically that his wound would always be aching when she left.

A month went by. He was still unsteady on his feet when one Sunday he wanted to go out with Mitis and Momi who came to see him almost every evening, a touching sign of how much they cared for him. He often scolded them: "Why do you come to see me? Don't you realize that I can't return your affection? That I'm not capable of friendship anymore? Leave me alone with my selfishness and indifference!" But Mitis understood why Pasini had shifted from his earlier childish effusiveness to this melancholy resignation. "Shut up," he said sharply. "You're not only an ingrate, you're also contradicting yourself; you've decided to live but you're throwing away life's one sure consolation, and that's friendship."

Lost in thought, Momi stared silently at the floor. They continued to come back, night after night. They would talk to him about what was happening at school. Among other things, they told him about Antero's month-long leave of absence due to nervous exhaustion. Pasini had withdrawn into himself; for some time now the image of Antero had been haunting his memory; countless things about him that he'd barely noticed seemed filled with meaning now that he was revisiting them: his breaking away from his friends, the distance he deliberately kept from the group that circled around Edda, the "lei" that he alone in the class would use in addressing her—although when he thought no one was looking, he would cast confidential, passionate looks her way; all that seemed proof that Antero was in love with Edda, and in love with her in a different, more profound way than the others, maybe the same way he loved her. That would explain why his former friend had never even shown his face at his hospital room door to find out whether he was dead or alive. A great fondness for Antero was being rekindled in his heart. He wanted very badly to see him again. His month of leave would be over in a few days, so he'd see him again at school, because he was going to go back too. By this time he'd decided to sit for the exams and in fact wanted to take his chances at the first session, so that once and for all and as fast as he could, he'd be out of that school where he'd suffered so for eight years and whose recent tragic months especially were hanging heavily over him.

They met up again at school. As it happened, they both went back on the same day and ran into each other in the atrium. Pasini was with Mitis. Antero had changed; he had put on weight and his pinker complexion went strangely well with his new light-colored summer suit; he looked fresh from the tailor and the barber.

"Well, look who's here!" Mitis laid into him. "You've gone middle-class on us!" he added in disdain.

Instead of replying, Antero reached out to shake Pasini's hand, looked him in the eye with affectionate concern, and said kindly:

"How are you, Pasini? I'm sorry I wasn't brave enough to come talk to you or write you before; but believe me, I've been suffering too and I understand what you've been going through."

Pasini peered at his friend's face; he seemed sincere. He hugged him.

"My old friend," he said to him, "I think we've both changed, you because of all the fresh forest air you took in, me because I've reacquired a taste for life. But maybe the two of us are the only ones who can understand what's going on inside us. What a mess we both are underneath our new façades!"

*****

School was almost over. Flustered by the turbulent flow of life beyond the breakwater of their studies, the seniors were obsessed with the looming exams and how serious they were, and this had reestablished their earlier sense of boundaries and order. Their preoccupation with studying and grades—which this time really did matter—had restored the collegial gaiety that had seemed banished forever from Edda's class. Once again, after such a long time, all its members were in attendance. All of them, unconsciously or on purpose, were doing their best to avoid new arguments and to forget about old ones; each one of them knew or intuited that this was the last stretch left in their adolescence that they could spend together as a group.

One day, fun-loving Vitelli piped up, "Okay. By this time, we've produced enough long faces to write a world-class tragedy. Could we please get going once again on our comedy?"

"Well, you'll have to play Pulcinella," answered Mitis.

Everybody laughed. Their collective laughter, something that for some time hadn't been heard in class, after a moment of shocked surprise, got them all going.

"Careful. If he hears the word 'baboon,' he goes bananas." It was Turez tossing out his first wisecrack of the year.

"More bananas than this?" Saletti gurgled in the midst of more laughter.

"Quiet, here comes the Bab...*oon*," shouted Marzi who'd stuck his head out the door, leaning hard on the "o's." This time their laughter shook like a thunderclap.

The "Baboon," that is, the professor of philosophy, burst into class purple with repressed rage.

"Where on earth do you think you are?" he yelled, "In some infernal madhouse?"

"The mouse had fallen in with wicked cats!" Turez, straight-faced in the last row, whispered out Dante's verse from the *Inferno*.

Trying to conceal their repressed laughter, their heads bobbed up and down like a field of wind-blown wheat.

"Somebody here is going to pay the price for all of you!" The professor, furious, shouted once more.

Silence.

"That's a fine seriousness," he went on. "Nobody studies here. All year long you're slackers; at the end, right at exam time, when you should be getting your heads together, you lose them completely. Has anybody ever heard such a racket? Not even kids somewhere out in the street."

"Have some respect, dog breath!" Laughter again, even more repressed. The teacher either didn't hear or pretended not to and he began the lesson.

The class seemed rejuvenated. There was no way that merry morning could come to an end without a good loud chorus as a finale. And a chorus there was, so mighty it scandalized the whole school; the teachers came running and so did the principal, who threatened severe punishments, including cancelling the July exams and holding everybody back until October. But clemency prevailed and the whole thing was blamed on the heat and on anxiety about the exams.

*****

During the break between the last class and the start of exams, Mitis's room was turned into a real general headquarters. In shirtsleeves, all day every day, Antero, Mitis, Pasini, and Momi gathered there around a table covered with dictionaries, Latin and Greek texts, history books, and atlases. One or another of them would ask in turn about a difficult passage, seek an answer to a knotty question, complain about the excessively demanding program. Every once in a while, Mitis's mother, a quiet, unassuming, middle-aged woman, would bring refreshments. And then, if only the four of them were there, they would stop studying and talk about other things, for example, what their futures might hold. Mitis was inclined toward journalism; he was going to take up law, but as soon as he could, he wanted to enter the political fray: his ideas were quite clear … Italy needed to declare war on Austria. Pasini didn't know what his life was going to hold: "I'd like to go to Paris," he said, "and live day to day on poverty and utopias; I'm never going to accomplish anything in life."

"No," Antero interrupted. "Go ahead and talk like that if you want to, but I think that life demands we accomplish something."

"But what? What?" Pasini retorted sharply.

"It doesn't matter if I don't know exactly what," responded Antero, "I just feel—and I really could sense this over and over again during that month when I was able to think for a while—that we're put here to work hard and to suffer."

Mitis agreed, Pasini shook his head, not persuaded; Momi said nothing.

"Say something, Momi," urged Antero clapping him on the shoulder.

"If there were a God," he finally muttered, "life wouldn't be so senseless! Anyhow, I'm thinking of going to work in the mines; the further underground we are, the fewer clouds there are for us to lose ourselves in." Momi had never spoken at such length and all of them listened in amazement.

In came Edda.

"Honestly, if this heat keeps up much longer, I'm not going to take the exams; I'll be dead first. And there's so much to study that I feel like giving up the whole thing!"

"Good girl," said Mitis. "You're always the voice of doom and gloom, and then at the exams you'll beat the pants off all of us!"

"Do you remember your exams at the beginning of the year?" Antero added. "It seemed like you were going to fail in every area but instead ..."

"All of you think I'm faking it? Well, test me in history; you'll see that I don't know anything anymore; my head is completely upside down."

"When did Fredrick the Second die?" Pasini started grilling her immediately.

"In 1250."

"And the Battle of Lepanto?"

"1571."

"And the Treaty of Lunéville?"

"1801."

"Enough, cut it out," Mitis and Antero interrupted in unison.

Edda pulled the other chair up to the table and sat down.

"Whose half-finished lemonade is this?" she asked, raising the glass and holding it up to the light.

"It's Momi's," Pasini answered.

"Momi, in fact, has always been the most generous of all of you; you complain that people never give you anything and meanwhile you drain your glasses, while Momi doesn't say a word but leaves half of his for thirsty newcomers." And she took a sip at the drink.

"Drink it up, Marty," said Momi, who seemed quite another person in all this. "That may be the last swallow you'll ever take with all the rest of us. Three months from now when we're scattered throughout the world, some in Florence, some in Paris, some in Vienna, you'll barely remember what our last names are."

Edda Marty shook her head: "No, none of you, not even you, Momi, have ever caught on to who I am. You've never understood me. All I wanted was to be your friend, and you've constantly rejected me, stuffing me into a gender category; you've forced me to be nothing except a woman so that I would be able to get under your skin."

Pasini was getting nervous. "It's easy for all of you to talk so calmly; you seem so many Olympic gods; but I'm just a poor mortal whose wound still hurts. I can't wait to get out of here. And maybe I really could forget each one of you, even your last names."

Antero had stood up; he wanted to cut the conversation short because he was finding it futile and distressing; as far as he was concerned, that year had been the first big disappointment of his life; he intended to move on from there. "Come over here, come take a look!" he called them. "There's a huge red cloud floating up in the sky!"

*****

Suddenly the air grew leaden; the first drops of rain began to fall, making big splashes on the pavement. Then, without warning, way up high the sky split open and between flashes of lightning and thunderclaps that shook the building and made the windows rattle, an unbelievable storm began to rage with hailstones the size of walnuts. The streets were covered by a gorgeous, crackling white carpet; roofs and eaves shone as if covered with glass.

Leaning out the window, Edda gathered handfuls of hailstones and handed them out to the others.

"Hey! Mitis, Momi!" Someone was yelling out in the street.

Everyone looked out. Below, soaking wet and happy were Zottig and Saletti and some other schoolmates who were looking up, all smiles. "Hurry," they shouted. "The school's been flooded! A bunch of teachers are trapped inside."

They went down at a run. It was quite a spectacle. Almost all the lower streets, close to the sea, had been turned into muddy torrents with some of the hailstones still floating on top. The school looked like an island. From the ground floor windows, teachers were peering out—some disconsolate, some contrite, some amused—all of whom seemed to be saying, "Just look at what those of us who have to maintain respectability are forced to put up with!"

Directly in front of the main door a crew had piled onto a big makeshift boat and was waving their arms at them, quick to jeer and make fun of any of the besieged who might be brave enough to try to escape.

The arrival of Edda and the others, wading in water up to their knees, was welcomed with hurrahs of jubilation. Fifty arms pulled them up onto the "vessel," one of those long, narrow carts normally used for selling citrus fruit that had been dragged up onto the sidewalk.

"Put Mitis in command," everybody yelled.

"Okay, all of you," Mitis began to announce. "We're pirates, but kind-hearted ones. Let's four or five of us get out and pull the boat to the other shore and take on board the stranded ..."

"Farties ... Warties ..." were suggested to great guffaws.

"Quiet! Let's rescue the stranded ... *Parties* and ferry them over to dry land."

The proposal wasn't unanimously welcomed, some protesting that they didn't deserve it, that they should be left there and go without their dinners... But ten willing helpers were already in the water and had started to drag the cart toward the school.

Between encouragements and refusals, a lot of negotiation was necessary before the teachers, mastering their own reservations, allowed themselves to be put on the cart. And when it began to move, more than one of them was worried about ending up head over heels in the quagmire. But Mitis skippered the craft with skill and devotion.

"What on earth are you doing here?" asked the professor of Greek, marveling once the first fear had passed when he noticed Edda.

"Here? I'm everywhere, Professor, wherever I can raise a ruckus with my friends," she shot right back.

"Well, well, well," sighed the Baboon, "how mistaken our judgments sometimes are!"

"Professor, Professor," called Zottig from the side rail of the cart, wading through the water up to his knees, "after all my efforts!" Gesticulating madly, he started to shout, "The exam question, come on, the exam question in philosophy. I've earned it!"

"So, you rascal, I'll give you your exam question in philosophy!"

And so, before much longer, propelled by a gale of high spirits, the passengers were able to disembark at the first dry spot. The cart was returned. The group broke up hoping for an even bigger storm the following day, the first day of their exams.

*****

With the exceptions of Zottig and Turez, who were held back until October, all the others passed the exams and graduated, including Pasini. Their final banquet went down into the annals of student history as one of the best and most uproarious of all time.

At this point, with some of them scattered into the mountains, others gone off to the shore, still others on longer excursions, the group that was still in Trieste had thinned out. Antero joined his family in a town on the Istrian coast where his sailboat was waiting for him. Momi and Mitis went off with hiking boots and sleeping bags to tour the whole region of Cadore on foot. Pasini, reluctantly, went with his sister to a destitute village high in the Carso in order to recuperate. Edda vomited a considerable amount of blood and nearly died; barely out of bed, she insisted on embarking on a long trip to the Orient. Neranz stayed where he was; every day at noon and sunset he would stroll down the Corso, hooking up with whomever he met and sharing stories about Edda: even some greybeard professors with families had fallen for her; and, perfectly capable of taking on four or five at a time, she had run through every one of them; a real teenage tart.

"Go figure," he would always conclude, "she tried to lasso even me. 'Do you want to marry me, Neranz?' she once asked. 'Me marry you? I'd hang myself first!'" And as he prepared to burst into laughter, he would loosen his arm from that of his companion, take both hands, and clamp his glasses tight to his tiny little nose.

The Island

(1941)

The little white steamer moved out of the port. The amphitheater of the city, swirling away in the distance, was an enchanting pink vision in the early morning sun. Already, the air was quivering with the heat. Once out of the port, it was easier to breathe. The azure color of the open sea, dusted with golden light, embraced the trustingly determined prow. All the passengers were on deck to enjoy the spectacle.

The son could feel the old pleasure of sailing reawakening within him. He had left his mountains with a certain regret. But his father had written asking that he make that sacrifice for him; perhaps for one last time. The unusual tone of the letter, the words solemn with pain, had surprised and concerned him.

That day he had come back a bit late; at the other tables people were eating; beyond the big, mullioned windows the peak of the Croda Rossa rose imposingly in the clear air; the waitress had freshened the flowers on his table with a big bunch of yellow monk's hood. He was still overheated from the climb down, his heart full of joy and his eyes filled with the sight of the rocky crests and ice formations; he had a few splendid edelweiss in his hand.

Among the correspondence on the table he saw the letter from his father and, still standing, he read it right away. What his father wrote was very touching: he wanted to go back to the island where he had been born and spend a few peaceful days there, maybe his last ones, and he would be grateful if his son would be able to go with him …

After he put the letter down, his fingers were trembling as he placed the edelweiss in the vase next to the monk's hood. The two young Viennese women at the neighboring table asked him admiringly where he had picked them, but his mind was already elsewhere.

He knew that his father's days were numbered. But could these really be his final ones? "He might last another year or so, you never know …" He had often dismissed the thought of such a premature death. But now the letter was casting a cold shadow onto his heart. Outside, the sun was shining gloriously on the meadows, on the peaks, on the fields of snow.

He had made up his mind instantly and quickly packed his bags. With the sun high in the sky, he went down the steep path through the forest of ancient fir trees, made it to the bus just in time, then caught the train at the tidy, deserted alpine station, and arrived in the city early in the morning of the following day.

Now he was strolling along the deck of the boat. His blood, accustomed to the mountain air, pulsed heavily in his wrists and temples, but he was already adapting to the sea. Even his eyes were suffering less from the glare and relentless glittering of the blue water. It was his sea: the vast reign of his adolescent years, his refuge, the friend of his earliest youth. All he needed was the smell of the sea to re-experience an almost carnal connection with that immense liquid body that had held him up countless times, pushed him under, and welcomed him back. As the ship moved forward, the constant breeze with its salty aroma was making him giddy, as though he were breathing in a deeper, more exhilarating way.

As he was walking back and forth, his father was sitting right there on a folding chair, leaning back against the wall of the little deck cabin. He smiled when he saw him come over. But his face was now marked with indelible sadness. His shoulders seemed to be working hard to support a body that would have collapsed without the firm determination still controlling it.

Was this the man who twenty years earlier had taken him on another boat to Dalmatia?

Every time he thought about the trip to Dalmatia, he relived the feelings of that event; it was a dark, physiological sensation: maybe the way a butterfly feels when it leaves the chrysalis.

He had set out with his slender shoulders muffled in a gray overcoat; the visor of a little cap over his forehead let him conceal the sickly timidity of the ten-year-old boy that he was then: thin, and pale as a new-born shoot that has grown up in the shade, with frightened eyes brimming with an embarrassed curiosity about himself. A month later, he had come back a different person: his chest strengthened, his head held high, confident, and at ease with his own instincts. The world no longer consisted of his shabby house, his elementary school building, the public park, and the few adjacent streets; in it there were cities and countries, steamships, and trips to be taken. He could feel fresh, new blood pulsing in his veins; his eyes looked out with a new frankness. He had gotten to know the sea and learned to trust it. He had been in contact with men who, despite his age, had treated him with respect. And he had looked in a calm, fearless way into the eyes of women: beautiful, elegant women who returned his greeting or waved their perfumed arms toward his face to say in Croatian: "laku noc" – good night.

All of that he owed to his father. He had seemed like a god to him then, powerful, with his beaming face, his resonant voice, his conquistador's manner: forthright, simple, merry. Under his guidance, he had learned how to handle himself and there, where at first he had imagined only unknown and frightening abysses, he had discovered solid ground and the joy of treading on it unconcerned. "I'm going to take care of some business, you look around, take a walk, enjoy yourself. We'll see each other again at such and such a time …"

And now that god was leaning his back and neck against a wooden wall, letting himself be rocked in his exhaustion by the quiet motions of the boat.

Filled with melancholy, his eyes were tracing the distant profile of the coast, out of focus and with blue and pinkish lights and tiny houses like flocks of sheep clustered here and there around the bell towers next to the still waters of the inlets. Now he was just an exhausted man with deep wrinkles in his face, his mouth forlorn and sagging half-open, as if it hurt him to breathe.

*****

The father watched his son coming along the passageway toward him on the deck: he stopped to say a few words to him, pointing out a couple of the little towns along the coast and they talked together about happy memories. Then he watched him go back toward the front of the boat, his slender, well-proportioned frame silhouetted against the background of sea and sky: a young man in the prime of his life. He was concerned that he might be bored; in the mountains—which he'd left for his sake—his son was maybe happier than he was at sea. He couldn't understand such a preference: mountains had always seemed gloomy to him. But his son was different; he had to recognize that. And it touched him to think that he'd agreed at once to take those few days and keep him company at the seaside.

He'd sensed for some time that he wasn't the same man he once was. Something in him was giving way. Was the end point that he'd never wanted to think about drawing near? Even now, it seemed pointless to be thinking about it; but he was thinking about it, his mind going there, painfully, and more and more often.

Difficulty in breathing, a chill coursing through his veins, he had never experienced such things before. Though now, on the boat, he felt fine. When he closed his eyes, all he could feel was the brisk air and the hot sun. All of life's other comforts had little by little abandoned him: the only things left were the shining sun of those splendid, cloudless days, the vivid skies from dawn to dusk— and the affection of his son.

He was on good terms with that son of his, almost as if he'd run into him by accident: as though he'd discovered some part of himself that he hadn't been aware of before.

A good many years had gone by since then. His son was still a child when he'd found himself face to face with him during one of his quick trips back to the family. That child with the fearful, imploring eyes in the big kitchen, beneath a sooty oil lamp, had been a surprise for him.

Up to then, he hadn't felt tied to anyone. His relationship with the family had been based on mutual indifference. Habitually, as sailors do, after his long trips, he would now and again go back to a home where it would seem he'd left behind some personal object, or some memories, but nothing alive, nothing that was really a part of him. Though one day, he discovered that there was a connection between the fearful, imploring eyes of that child and his own soul that he could no longer ignore, much less dismiss except at the cost of considerable pain. That was why he had first accepted that little son into his own world and then taken him by the hand and shown him how to find his own way through life.

Now, it was true, he could see him moving through life confidently—and he was proud of that. He was glad that he was different from him and that the path he'd chosen was loftier and more straightforward than the one he'd taken. The comparison didn't bother him. He had no regrets about how he'd lived his life. Looking back on it, his life seemed a boisterous sailing trip, and the ports where he'd landed had been fertile vineyards full of grapes that he had plucked at just the right moment, neither unripe nor shriveled and dry. He had had a very good time. Now the grapevines were bare, with only a few stubborn grape leaves still attached to the branches; but they were already feeling the first tugs of the winter wind ...

"Are you hungry?" he asked his son when he came over to him.

"A little. But, will you be able to eat on board?"

"Sure. The first mate knows who I am and already knows which dishes are going to work out for me. The usual pap."

*****

The son was pacing back and forth again. He had looked away just in time not to reveal how upset he was. He couldn't forget the smile that seemed to confirm his father's last words, nor the look in those eyes when he lifted them to meet his. A smile of infinite sadness, of stoic resignation; though not in his eyes: somewhere in the depths of those eyes that were trying so hard to appear earnest, an infantile terror was glittering.

Did his father know he was dying? Was he aware that his illness was fatal? The letter he'd sent to him in the mountains, the tone of certain things he said, his air of smiling resignation made him think that he was. But his determination to see his island again, maybe for the last time; before leaving, his having put together some new fishing tackle (how proud he had been to show it to him!); certain nostalgic glances: all those things might be gleams of a hope that wouldn't give up.

Across the sea, all the way to the horizon, scattered white and orange sails collected the sun like mirrors; hovering seagulls following the boat just overhead beat their wings and then dipped down into its wake; small boats steamed along the coast moving comically about like toys; all this dominated from on high by an enormous sky pallid with intense light.

This is what the son could see physically; but another inner vision, cold and unyielding, almost ghost-like, was superimposing itself on these sprawling panoramas, blurring the clarity of the world and casting a malevolent shadow on the pleasure of being alive. Even when he was up in the mountains, such a vision had sometimes darkened his thoughts. He would push it away, dispatching it to the recesses of his mind, but it resurfaced insistently.

The smooth, cold, metallic office of a radiologist. A pale torso naked inside the machine, a worried but resigned face topping the screen. Sudden darkness; the buzz and violet flashes of the apparatus; nothing but the bright, sinister screen. And on the screen the indistinct skeletal outline of the thorax. The voice of the doctor: "Hold it in your mouth, swallow when I tell you; swallow!" And there moving down the thorax from top to bottom, a small gray ball that kept on going until it suddenly stopped, as if it had reached the base of a sack, where it started to dissolve, shrank to something string-like, and then disappeared ...

Before he could see his father's wasted face in the light above the machine again, he had been frightened on down to his very roots: just like a young plant when it feels a fatal slash cutting off its connections with the earth. In such a moment of suspended time, beyond all contingencies, horrified, his mind lucid, his whole being frozen in time, he had had looked death in the eye: what he had seen on that screen was a part of himself.

To drive away that haunting vision and avoid running into his father every time he went back toward the cabin, the son was careful to limit his walks to the passageway on the other side of the boat.

Here there were various people who distracted him a bit. Earlier some children playing tag had bumped against his legs: now he saw them clustered around their mother who was sitting on a lounge chair and must have been telling some marvelous stories, waving her pale hands at imaginary creatures as she stared out somberly onto the expanse of the sea beyond her children's heads. All of them had dark, almond-shaped eyes, which were shining and intent.

An elegant, elderly gentleman seated further forward was leafing through some illustrated magazines while savoring a cigar, moving it away every now and again and making the ashes fall off with little rhythmic taps of his slender index finger. A tall, thin priest was walking in the opposite direction and when they crossed paths, the priest would smile at him, almost as if he'd have liked to say something.

How easily all those people breathed and moved. But to him they seemed like many thoughtless actors declaiming their lines on a stage, and unaware of what was lurking behind them. Wasn't a person who was at death's door traveling on the same boat with them? Death, lodged in the esophagus just at the third rib …

With the light switched back on, while his father was getting dressed in the adjacent room, the radiologist had made a quick sketch on a piece of paper: the tube of the esophagus and about halfway down, a constriction. He was speaking without emotion. A tumor, quite advanced. Treatment? None. Or rather… if you wanted to prolong the suffering for a few months, there was radiation. But even then, he might hold out a year or two; you never can tell …

It had started to happen the day after the visit to the doctor. Strolling along the streets of the city with his father on his arm, the world of humans seemed divided into two parts: in one sharply defined sphere he could see phosphorescent skeletons moving about; and in a second sphere that was extremely bright and unreal, as if superimposed on the first, he could see them dragging their ephemeral envelopes of flesh behind them. The sensation had been so profound and painful that he'd been afraid he would never be able to shake off its memory. But then, slowly, for him too, life had gone back to its usual deceptions.

*****

In the dining room, the large tables already set for diners gleamed beneath whirring ceiling fans. As they made their way down, the passengers seated themselves with that mixture of condescension and cheerful curiosity that makes meals on board, when the sea is calm, so agreeable. "It's like glass, just like glass": and they peered at each other, congratulating themselves one by one on the smooth sailing and the danger they'd been spared on a crossing that, at that point, was usually rough. "I've never—and I know what I'm talking about—seen the Gulf of Quarnero so calm," said the elegant, elderly man to the mother of the children, whose meaningful glances and monosyllables in an unknown foreign language were not sufficient to keep them as calm as the waters of the Quarnero.

Painfully concerned, the son kept one eye on his father seated next to him; he was edgy and wanted to spare him any sort of humiliation; he cast around for some topic that might distract him. But his father was at ease, smiling, pleased, almost, to be surrounded by the eager glances of those happily hungry people.

The waiters began to come around with trays, and in the sudden quiet of the room you could hear the whirring of the fans again; then, shortly afterward, there was the muffled sound of cutlery and desultory conversation. The diners were concentrating most of their attention on what they were eating, but every glance, even accidental ones, that the son saw directed toward his father's plate made him apprehensive.

One of the waiters stopped somewhat thoughtlessly behind his father and held out a tray; when he indicated that he didn't want any, he apologized. The mistake was a simple one, but it made his son blush. And he was also stung when he saw the head waiter motion toward his father from the back of the room and had him served out of turn with the meal that had been specially prepared for him: an event that aroused the curiosity of the nearby diners.

His father raised the food to his mouth slowly and swallowed with dissembled effort. It was difficult for him to get down even those skimpy bites of something soft that had been finely diced. Beneath the skin, his face muscles made it clear what an effort he was making; the tendons in his emaciated neck vibrated like cords strung too tight.

With what a robust appetite, with what healthy enjoyment the son remembered having seen his father eat at other ships' tables. In a good mood, his words flowing easily; no over-indulgence, a balanced moderation, a generous sense of the boundaries affecting pleasure and good health. It was as if everyone around him were subject to his whims, surrendering to that merry, convivial atmosphere. And the wine! Every time, he would raise his glass and savor it with his eyes before tasting it. What a wonderful way of drinking!

The same courtly table manners even now; but how it hurt his son to see those measured gestures, that careful attentiveness to what he was doing, that hesitant sipping of the wine in his glass.

The waiter who was serving the cream pie held out the tray and asked uncertainly, "Some of this?" His father smiled at the kind consideration and said no. He calmly lit a cigarette. His hands were trembling a bit, the ends of his fingers the color of burnt ivory.

His son felt choked with emotion. In his mind's eye, the fan spinning over the table was transformed into the old oil lamp hanging from the ceiling of the gloomy kitchen that lay at the center of all his childhood memories. In his imagination he could see the silver cigarette case with the tiny horse etched on it; he could see his miserable self again in the figure of the skinny boy sitting there alongside the table. They were all alone in the large, empty kitchen: he, filled with adoration, wonder, and fear; and, leaning over him, his face handsome with manly assurance, his father; the light from the oil lamp beat down on his blond moustache and onto his hand resting on the table: an aristocratic hand with fingertips the color of burnt ivory.

He was shaken out of his reverie. His father had reopened the cigarette case and was offering him a cigarette.

"No thanks. Are you smoking as much as ever, Papa?"

"Not so much anymore."

"And you started young, right?"

"As a boy. But you, you've never taken up the habit?"

"I don't really need it. Two, three cigarettes a day."

"It must be the mountain air that you like so much… Aren't you sorry you had to come down here from your mountains?"

"Oh, Papa."

"But you'll be able to go back; we won't stay on the island more than a couple of weeks. Just a brief respite … It was a sudden impulse, one of those sentimental urges you just know you can't say no to."

He smiled, his face at peace and free of bitterness.

"Then I intend to really get back to work. I haven't been very happy with myself lately: I've let myself get awfully lazy."

"But … you've been sick, Papa." His son could sense immediately how shallow his words had been.

"Well, life is almost over. Pretty soon I'll be at the end. But that's no excuse for idleness—on the contrary, in fact."

Once again, the suspicion that his father knew all about his illness kept him from answering and left him concerned. Maybe this was the right moment for him to say something just as clear and frank? But could he be certain that what his father's words really meant were: "I'm doomed," or maybe just vaguely "I've reached the sunset of my life and everybody knows that death is going to come in the end"? Hadn't he said, just a moment ago, that he was going to go back to work after their brief holiday?

"You don't have to work. Why do you want to wear yourself out?" But even as he said those words, the son could tell how meaningless they were. He knew that his father had always worked, in response to the same natural impulse that a plant does when it sends sap to its leaves; and even at the brink of death, it never ceases doing so; stopping would be to give up, accept death, even encourage it.

With mixed feelings of admiration and envy, the son turned to look at his father. He was peering into the distance through the smoke from his cigarette. They were almost alone in the dining room; the waiters were clearing the tables.

"Wear myself out? No, I get more tired when I start thinking about my condition, my illness."

"Once you're feeling better …" The lie faltered on his son's lips; though he was thinking how necessary, even if cruel, it was to probe a little. This was the moment to try to get through and see how his father really felt. Looking at him, he could see a faint blush move down his cheeks beneath the pallid flesh.

"I don't have much faith in doctors. So far, I haven't noticed that I'm getting any better. It does get harder and harder to swallow."

Hanging intently on every gradation in his father's voice, the son winced: how tellingly the expression "so far" had resonated amidst the blandness of the other things he had said.

"But I thought you ate well today."

"Right, today I feel better, much better."

This time it was his father who turned to look at his son: his gaze was tender and filled with gratitude. The son hung his head: he couldn't meet that look without letting on how he really felt.

"It's the sea air, your company, the pleasure of spending a few days on the island that are doing me good."

"Has it been a while since you were there last?"

"I think a lot about going, but there's always something that keeps me from it. I make do with sailing past, catching a glimpse, and dreaming about it like some memory from childhood. It's not the place it used to be. Every time I've gone back, I've been disappointed. It's been five or six years since the last time. Want to go up on deck?"

*****

The sea was endless now and glistened with every wave. In the distance, the horizon was blurred by a light haze. On the left, one could imagine rather than distinguish a faint outline of mountains in profile: but perhaps they were clouds. Nearly all the passengers were napping on the lounge chairs. The marine midday hung heavy in the breeze caused by the ship's movement: that inexpressible sense of wellbeing, that sensual anxiety that makes you want to keep to yourself, not say a word, commune with your private feelings.

But then the mountainous archipelago swam into view: a crystalline, indigo mass imbedded in the blue liquid of the sea. Caught by surprise, the passengers realized that they were just at the edge of the coast. The boat was sailing fast; the panting noise made by the propellers was now amplified by an echo. The sparse vegetation along the rocky bluffs, the all-white hamlets on the water's edge gave a special sense of freshness and enchantment to the land was emerging from the sea.

Brought back to life by the realization that they were arriving, many of the passengers had risen to their feet.

Once the boat entered the inlet, they thronged along the rail eager with curiosity: suddenly it seemed they were sailing across a lake and when they turned to look back, they could no longer tell where they had come in. A blissful tranquility hung over everything, making the boat seem suddenly lighter, barely supported by the water.

The island was outlined by gentle contours; a darker blue sky was peeping through the bluish tops of the olive trees; the still air was replete with a heady fragrance, and the smells of the earth were intermingled with the smells of the sea: pine, mint, and oleander with salt and seaweed.

At the end of the inlet, the little town climbed in terraces up to the hilltop dominated by the church. The houses there were old, gray, and peeling. Down on the shore there were bright splashes of color and the buildings were more modern.

Once they had run their gazes back down from the upper city, the father and son looked each other in the eye.

"Is that the one?" the son asked.

"Yes, it is. That's the house."

Falling silent, they turned again to look at a house at the top of the hill, its roof rising above the other roofs clustering around the church. On the other side of the roof, they could make out the foliage of a fig tree.

"They've let it go to rack and ruin," his father added after a moment. The tone of his voice was tinged with a regret that, to his son, seemed new and strange: it was the first time he had heard a note of bitterness in his father's words, a longing for things now over and gone.

The son had been in that house as a boy. An aunt of his father's was living there then. He remembered the cistern under the entryway beneath the house's foundation and how his footsteps would echo over that empty space. He remembered the vegetable garden just a few steps down; it was a forlorn, messy garden, with a fig tree in the center and a big caper plant on the wall—the only pretty thing in the garden. Even then, everything had an air of abandon and doom: the plaster was peeling off, the ceilings were cracked, the stones on the outside were worn and had come loose. The old woman, nearly blind, made her way by holding onto the wall with her hand. She had told him that in the attic there were likely to be some old books: her husband and son had been readers. He had gone up there hoping to unearth some treasure but all he found was a pile of tattered notebooks with worn pink paper; mice were rustling beneath them.

"Can't we go and stay up there?" asked the son hesitantly, realizing as he did so how silly his question had been. But he was glad that it made his father smile.

"The house is empty and falling down. And then four hundred and fifty stairs are just too many for someone as short of breath as I am. No, we want to take it easy these few days. I've already written to Teresa and asked her to get two rooms ready for us in her house. We'll be fine there. Maybe just one nuisance: the mosquitos. Since you've just come down here from the mountains, you're going to have a hard time with the heat at night."

How talkative his father had become! He was breathing more freely; he seemed healthy. Maybe the doctors had gotten it wrong? Maybe there was no malignant tumor and still some hope of his getting better?

While the boat was docking at the pier, in the cheerful bustle of the arrival, the son let himself be persuaded by that sweet and unforeseen sense of hope, however absurd. He slipped his arm underneath his father's and, though noticing its pitiful thinness, was imagining the moment when he would be able to announce to him with complete conviction: "You've gotten well, Papa." And, as if preparing for such a moment, he racked his brain for something to make his father feel better.

"You did right to call me down from the mountains. How beautiful the island is."

His father squeezed his arm in silent affection.

In the crowd that was waiting for them were a number of people who seemed surprised, and voices and hands greeted his father jubilantly. Once they had come down the gangplank, they crowded around to ask why on earth he hadn't been back for such a long time and shook their heads at his unannounced arrival. His son? What a surprise; they remembered what he had been like as a boy, but no one would be able to recognize him now.

His father smiled affably and joked that it had been the winds of old age that had blown him into port; that he had brought some new fishing tackle and intended to sit on the embankment, dangle his legs, and forget the world. It was clear from his tone that he was teasing them; and he was pleased by their protests, by their friendly cuffs on the shoulder.

A young boy made his way through the group and announced that Teresa was expecting them. She'd told him that he was to carry their suitcases.

Off they went, promising to meet up later at the café.

*****

Tall, her hair undone, wearing a flowered dressing gown that hung down over her thin angular body, with white tufts of hair sticking out of her bonnet, the elderly Teresa made her way toward them.

"Oh, finally, finally. What a pleasure to see you."

She took them right away to see the rooms she'd prepared for them.

"What a man your son has become. With a son like that, I hope you've grown up too. Your poor mother, may God keep her in glory, was always worried about you. You know, your father (now turning to the son) left the island early on. Of course, of course, who was there to look after him? He sailed out with the trade winds and that was good-bye for years and years. How many tears your poor grandma shed on this shoulder (and she tapped her shoulder). But do you like the rooms? Yes? I'm glad. Soon it'll be dinnertime. I've fixed some fish for you, boiled fish. You wanted it boiled, right? Oh, it's not the fish like there used to be. It's so hard to find any to buy these days, and ever since they built all those big hotels on the shore, you have to get down on your knees before they'll sell you any."

"She's a good woman," his father said once they were left alone. "Does her chatter bother you?"

His son said it didn't.

"Well, she is tiresome, but she's an odd woman. It depends on the day; sometimes she shuts down so completely there's no way you can pry a word out of her. And then she never sits at the table; she just stays in the kitchen. She's really just a poor old soul."

"Is she the one whose husband died during that dangerous rescue attempt?"

"Right, and her son in India of yellow fever. Disaster can really crush a family! I remember what a beautiful woman she was. Her husband had accustomed her to a life of ease and luxury; she needed afterwards to rent the house to tourists just to keep going. After her son died, she had to take care of the three grandchildren. She raised them all and insisted that they go to school, vowing to keep them far away from the sea. She can't bear to think about the sea, not even look at it through the window."

At the table they were joined by the widowed daughter-in-law and a grandson, a timid seminarian who'd come to spend his vacation with the family; the daughter-in-law, sickly, dressed for the occasion in something too tight for her, couldn't keep her squinty eyes and pale hands from fluttering around.

The room was filled with furniture, carpets, mats: old English porcelain, knick-knacks from Japan and India, prints, little models of sailing ships, exotic shells. It was like a bazaar: the typical house of a long-distance sailor. And the priest-to-be with his hangdog air and bony face lowered at an angle over his chest made a painful contrast with all those memories of past sailing trips; it was as if the robust trunk of the family, though accustomed to dangers and gales, at a certain point had snapped off and was now sprouting a slender twig that every gust of wind intimidated.

Surprised and happy, the son could see that his father was maintaining his good humor right through dinner and ate the soup and the fish with gusto, almost normally. No one, in fact, except for him, who knew what was going on, would have noticed the deliberation and pauses caused by his difficulty in swallowing. Even while he was eating, his father had tried to keep the conversation going and toward the end, thanks to him, the atmosphere had become quite relaxed. The seminarian, his eyes glowing and heaving heavy sighs, poured out confessions that made it clear that the seminary had yet to completely suffocate his ancestral sailor instincts; his mother, while describing her own misfortunes, no longer uncomfortable, had forgotten about her dress; and her hands and face, brought back to life by her memories of all she had gone through, now seemed almost pretty.

*****

The two rooms faced each other and were separated by a narrow hallway. Both had windows overlooking the port that lay just beyond a small triangular piazza. There in the middle of a struggling flowerbed under a palm tree stood the marble bust of a famous baritone, a favorite son of the island.

The heat was intense. The air hung over the port without stirring; it seemed to have absorbed all the warmth of the day in order to release it, relentlessly, into the night. Gusts of hot air streamed in through the half-open window.

The son, undressing in the dark and breathing heavily, was thinking back to the nights he had just left behind him. After dinner, he would go out. The thermometer would register only a few degrees above the red line marking the freezing point. On both sides of the pass, the mountains rose serene in their gloomy austerity; the air was unbelievably transparent; looking at the starry, frighteningly beautiful sky, he would feel almost dazed and begin to shiver. In the silence, the gentle sound of the rushing streams would bring him back to the fragrant earth. A sense of purity, like after a ritual bath, coursed through his veins. He would go back in and undress in the chilly, spruce-scented room, and once under his comforter, a light sleep would soon overtake him.

He leaned out the window. His father was at the neighboring window; his pointy shoulders and skinny arms stuck out of his undershirt; how sunken that once robust chest had become!

"How are you feeling?"

"Fine, I feel really good. But I'm worried that you, on the other hand, are not doing so well …"

"It's hot; I'll get used to it."

"Tomorrow morning, get up whenever you like and go off on your own. I've brought you to this island, I've caged you up on this rock; but now that you're here, you're free to do whatever you like; all I need to know is that you're somewhere nearby. We'll see each other at lunch. Don't worry about me."

The same kind consideration, almost the same words as on his first trip to Dalmatia: the son could feel his eyes grow moist with tears.

"Remember to light the chrysanthemum powder that I had you put on your bedside table; otherwise you won't sleep," his father added.

In fact, the clouds of mosquitos hovering in the light of the streetlamp on the piazza were already attracted by the odor of blood at the window. They swarmed around him with their soft perfidious buzz; every now and again one of them would hit against his cheek or ear; that irritating contact was amplified in his imagination; it was almost as if the slimy wing of some monster had brushed against his face.

He wished his father good night and leaned back in. He could tell that getting some rest was going to be difficult.

He tried to distract himself by thinking back about the cool nights and the silences up in the mountains, but his mind kept going blank or was weighed down by painful memories. His father was dominating his thoughts: his image of the vigorous, vital man whom he'd known in past years was merging with the exhausted person at death's door who was breathing so heavily on the other side of the hallway.

Now the images reversed themselves in his mind: he was the one who had fallen ill, while his father, sturdy as a well-built ship, had hold of him and was carrying him away in a brisk wind. The large room with monstrous shadows dancing in the flickering light of a candle; an awful darkness swallowing up his frightened spirit; a hammering pain in his head and the sense that he was losing control; a cry for help bursting from his chest, and the presence of his father more powerful and consoling than any beam of light might be; the terror ebbing, the pain subsiding, his spirit dissolving in a strange sweetness as he could feel the steady, strong chest of his father beneath his head; and so, transported and safe, he was falling peacefully to sleep.

But once in bed he couldn't sleep. The air had become even less breathable with the dense coils of smoke that sputtered up from the burning chrysanthemum powder on the table. Outside, the noises of the night were bothering him: footsteps, voices, the slapping of oars, whirring of propellers, and the revving of engines were thumping against the fibers of his brain.

*****

In the other room his father wasn't sleeping either. Nights were hard for him. Several times he got out of bed to pace the floor: when he lay down, he felt like a weight was crushing him. Even now on the island, though he'd been fine throughout the day, once night came he could feel that same dull, gnawing sensation: as though a dreadful crab that was thrusting its pincers into his flesh and, feeding on his tissues, was getting heavier and heavier and squeezing the life out of him. But his spirit was calmer and his mind serene and he didn't let it get the better of him. There he was on his island: sometimes he had wondered whether he would ever see it again.

He even smiled at himself in the dark when he thought back to the faces and comments made by the "old timers" who had approached him the moment he arrived and with whom he'd chatted at the café after dinner. How monotonous and disagreeable their lives must have been. He didn't envy them. A man born on the island was supposed to get out into the world and come back only at the end. Someone who had crossed the Atlantic fifty times or sailed on the Pacific, someone who had witnessed the fitting out of ships in the dry docks of Europe and America would never settle for looking out from an herb garden as the clouds rolled by overhead or, lolling in a little boat, gazing at the still waters of the port. Such a person would risk turning out like Fabrizio: with that long, pale face and its droopy skin and those watery eyes, he seemed like a rabid old mastiff tethered to a chain who had never been more than a couple of yards away from its kennel; or like Antonio, toothless, his chin forever resting on the knob of his walking stick, his eyelids red and lumpy, looking like someone who belonged in the poor house.

No, they wouldn't get him to become a part of their grouchy group; all he would need, when the time came, was the tiny plot where his father was buried: that was where he was going to rejoin the infertile earth of his native island, with his name engraved under that of his father on the modest slab of stone quarried from that same earth. Was his time growing near? Knowing whether it was or not wasn't important. A few good days did lie ahead, days that would be spent in the air he had breathed since infancy and that he felt belonged to him every bit as much as the blood that was pulsing in his veins.

Simple thoughts and quiet moments danced through his imagination. This to the extent that his physical condition didn't really bother him: it was like some tedious past that was growing more and more detached from real life.

He knew that over there, in the other, nearby room, his son lay breathing. This gave him a new and reassuring feeling of security. He had never felt the need to lean on anyone, but now a mysterious dread, buried somewhere deep inside him, was making him cast about as if looking for someone to encourage him. His son! Even though they didn't have much to say to each other, how easy it was for them to feel connected.

*****

Old Teresa, her hair still undone, came into the son's room to bring him breakfast. He asked about his father.

"Oh, he's already gone out. He's an early riser. What a man, so full of life and energy! He was feeling happy; I've always known him to be a happy and positive person. He said he'd meet you here for lunch. We eat at half past noon; but if you'd like it to be a bit later…"

"Did my father seem in good shape to you?"

"A little bit thinner than last time; but strong, solid as an oak."

The son did not answer. "Right," he thought, "an oak tree rotten to the core: it spreads out its limbs, the wind rushes through its leaves, but suddenly, presto, it crumbles to pieces and crashes to the ground."

"I wonder if his stomach is giving him trouble," Teresa added. "He's asked me to make him only broth and to mince up his meat … 'like something for a toothless old man,' he said. But he's still got beautiful, healthy teeth; 'it's probably just stress,' I told him. 'You have to stop thinking you're still a twenty-year-old; you have a grown son who could've given you a half-dozen grandkids, if he'd wanted to.' Though you're doing the right thing, you're right not to marry."

She burst into laughter and her whole skinny body began to shake under her dressing gown.

A sudden breeze swept over the port. The more breathable air, with its sharp salty aroma, made the son decide to go for a swim.

He knew the island well: on other trips, he had walked all across it and sailed around it too. He especially liked certain rugged, rocky slopes planted with olive trees—briny and perfumed with horehound, beaten by the winds, with the open sea in front and an endless sky to the back. The uninhabited part of the island was even better, with neither houses nor palm trees, just the tiny dry flowers of the sage plants and the bristly junipers; where the sea pounded among the cliffs or came to a calm in pretty little natural inlets.

When he left that morning, he was intending to see if he could find one of those secluded nooks to swim in. He remembered that not too far away, where the houses came to an end beyond the boatyards, the terrain narrowed and made a mounded isthmus: on one side the gulf, on the other and close to it, the open sea. The water was very deep and there were sharks in it that were attracted by the tuna traps nearby. No one ever swam in that area.

When he got to the other side of the isthmus, he was suddenly greeted by a powerful wind; he would never have imagined it could be so strong. All at once, he could feel the moist salt on his mouth and all over his body. Looking out over the endless expanse rough with foaming breakers, he was enveloped by the booming tumult of the waves pounding on the cliffs. Once he had taken a few steps forward, the spray came up to where he was standing.

What a contrast between the peacefulness of the gulf, protected on every side and inviting you to utter laziness, and that ridge that was completely exposed to the immense power of the sea. It was clear how determined and persistent the force had been that had created the island: this fistful of earth, in the midst of the furies and caprices of indomitable nature, constantly in danger of being smashed to bits, ripped from its moorings, and carried off triumphantly like some rotten hulk.

Now the son could better understand the character of the men who were born on the island, those who had could feel its structure in their bones and its restlessness in their blood; now he could understand his father better. The tranquility of the port was only an illusion; reality lay out there, in unabashed, perpetual struggle.

Excited by that liquid, blustery immensity, shot through with light and resounding with a powerful din, he found the mountains puny by comparison and he smiled at the memory of the arguments with his father who couldn't accept it that the mountains meant more to him than the sea did.

He picked out a sort of niche sheltered by two big rocks and undressed. He walked cautiously over that rough carpet of stones. Every now and again he could feel the chilly, tickling dampness of the foam between his toes; the wind was ruffling his hair and he felt pleasantly dazed; with his eyes half-closed he turned his face toward that overwhelming glare. But he felt sturdy and when he got slammed by the waves and had to struggle to keep from getting pushed over backwards, he enjoyed the feel of vigor and health coursing through his body. He went out through the breakers into the open sea, relishing going under and wrestling with such an implacable element: he knew that no weakness on his part would be forgiven.

When he turned back to look at the shore, he could see a figure standing on a rock.

His father. His bare head, round and with short, thin hair, rose proudly over his torso; his jacket and his trousers were being pummeled by the wind, but underneath, his body stood firm and upright. Who knows how long he'd been there, following him silently with his eyes. In the midst of all that glare, he seemed taller, younger. He had the strange impression that he was trying to compete with him. Standing there, on the solid surface of that rock whipped by the wind, he seemed his equal. The man who just yesterday had sailed on the boat leaning back against the wall of the ship's cabin was no longer recognizable.

With his sharp, attentive gaze carefully focused, his father's face had contracted a bit around the eyes because of the glare and the wind, but his smile grew broader and broader as his son drew near.

"Careful!" he shouted: there was no concern in his voice, he was just trying to warn him.

In fact, a more powerful wave did surprise his son from behind and bounced him toward the cliff. He just had time to turn around and get his feet on the bottom so he could fend off the impact by using his back and swinging his arms.

Once it had rolled back out, the wave left him upright and dripping with foam.

"Papa, how did you manage to find me?" he panted, still breathing hard from the swim.

"I guessed. You're a daredevil. No one from the island would have taken such a chance: there are always sharks prowling around here. But how gorgeous the open sea is. Good for you." His father's contented glance came to rest on his son's well-built body that the seawater had left burnished like a bronze statue.

"Have you ever gone swimming here?" With a few deft hops from rock to rock, his son had jumped up onto the overhang where his father was standing.

"Sure, in my day; I liked coming here even on stormy days," said his father, speaking calmly and without bravado, almost as if what he was saying was "it's your turn now." Then, laying a hand on his son's damp, glistening shoulder, he added, "the mountain has turned you all tan, the seaside sun will finish the job."

"That should be some contest," his son laughed. "But how did you spend the morning?"

"I had a look at the shoreline and picked out the spot where I'll go fishing this evening. I also checked out a few spots where everything has stayed just as it was when I was a boy. When you get old, it feels good to reassure yourself that the world hasn't changed completely."

"Have you turned into a philosopher, Papa?"

"That's something that comes with age; if you're not a philosopher when you're young, you turn into one later on."

*****

In the oppressive torpor of the afternoon, the son was dreaming about the thin, clean air of a siesta in the mountains: stone pines and larches were creating an island of shade on a gentle, grassy slope; a calm light wind was blowing down from the high meadows and working its way into the swaying branches of those age-old trees, blending into their resinous aromas the fragrance of monk's hood and vanilla orchids. But now, contrasting with those images, his imagination broadened out onto that morning's vision of the open sea, and his skin re-experienced the vigorous encounter with the liquid immensity of the water and the light. His groggy brain flickered back and forth between the pleasures of the mountains and the excitement of the sea.

But now a dull, persistent pain was added to that heavy mugginess. He could see his father again, just as he was a moment ago at the table: animated, relaxed, injecting life into everything around him, even the objects packed into that fusty room. Suddenly he turned silent: bent over his plate, his neck rigid, he had turned purple. To the astonishment of the widow and the seminarian, who up to then had been encouraging him, he had to get up and leave. After a bit, he came back, ashen, and with his eyes dazed and watery; thanks to a few witty quips, he had reestablished the earlier atmosphere, but he hadn't taken another bite.

Half asleep, the son was now reliving the horror of that moment when, without warning, illness had seized his father by the throat. That whole glorious, cloudless morning, one of those that makes the spirit brim over with joy and optimism, had suddenly been darkened by the symptoms of the illness that was constantly lying in ambush: the lightening-like proof of a reality from which there was no escape.

Life was coming to pieces: the cold pallor of death was concealed behind the transparency of vital, exuberant health; at the end of a sun-filled day enjoyed in the freedom of light and wind, lay stagnation, a suffocating closeness, where the brain dissolved and the spirit was fermenting with fear. A sense of uncertainty and of a miserable compromise with fatality was taking over everything.

Why, in such happy and harmonious circumstances, when he and his father had met on the rock, hadn't a more powerful wave carried them off and dragged them under? Their end would have arrived like a violent act of grace that would have spared them from being pulled under later by delusions of recovery and demeaning farewells.

He wasn't denying the inevitability of death, but he was rebelling at the tragic struggle between a sound and healthy organism and a cruel and insidious illness.

A struggle whose outcome had already been decided. And without any glimmer of hope. Once again, he could see that the waning light in his father's dazed eyes foreshadowed defeat. Perhaps, however, the person struggling isn't fully aware of how inevitable defeat is and for that reason can resist and find the strength to keep up the battle. If the blood running through his veins is the same as the victim's, however, the helpless observer of that tragic struggle will suffer with repressed horror, his every moment filled with bitterness.

Later, exhausted by the heat and his inner turmoil, the son left his room and knocked apprehensively at the door across from his. When no one answered, he opened it slowly. The room was still filled with smoke that was going out the window in lazy spirals through the half-opened shutters; on the table, the ashtray was filled with cigarette butts and spent matches and beside it, organized neatly in a tin box, was the new fishing tackle made from black horsehair lines wound around bobbers with shiny fishing hooks stuck in them. In some places there were empty spaces, perhaps for those his father had decided to take with him. "I had a look at the shoreline and picked out the spot where I'll go fishing this evening," he had said up on the rock, standing tall and with his eyes shining.

On the bedside table were his glasses and a gilt-edged book bound in black: the *Bible*. An old, illustrated parchment bookmark stuck out from the pages marking a passage from the *Book of Job*!

"Wherefore then hast thou brought me forth out of the womb? Oh that I had given up the ghost, and no eye had seen me!

"Are not my days few? Cease then, and let me alone, that I may take comfort a little;

"Before I go whence I shall not return, even to the land of darkness and the shadow of death."

The son's eyes, once they had lit on these verses, filled with tears. He would never have imagined that his father read the *Bible*. Ever since he had tagged along with him as a boy, he'd never seen very many books in his hands: a few travel books, some historical novels.

The room he'd entered had disclosed something intimate about his father's life that he never would have imagined. He knew his father as a man among other men. He knew what he was like in their own relationship, but only now was he beginning to see what he was like when he was by himself.

After a cheerless lunch, they had gone up to their rooms and parted without saying anything further. As he opened the door to his room, his father had smiled at him reassuringly. The same smile of boundless melancholy, of stoic resignation that on the steamer had tugged at his heart. After that, his father had stretched out on the bed and began to smoke.

How many depressing thoughts were contained in those blue spirals of smoke. Unable to sleep, he'd put on his glasses, and looked in the open *Bible* for the *Book of Job*; maybe he had just picked up where he left off. That passage must have provided him with a little peace. When he got up, he had gone to check on his fishing tackle: he had taken the lines from the box one by one, weighed them in his hands, tested the resistance of the line and the leaders; he'd wrapped them in a piece of cloth and crept out very slowly, without making any noise, so as not to awaken the son asleep in the other room.

This was how the son painfully evoked and pieced together the time his father had spent in his room and what he had done there, but he couldn't manage to tear himself away. It was almost as if a deeper revelation was destined to emerge for him from those simple objects, that smoke, the meager traces still lingering there.

*****

The sun was setting behind the low silhouette of the cliff that sheltered the port like an embrace. The pale light still in the sky was discomfortingly melancholy. It was a strange sunset: just a few colors, barely covered by a golden haze; the sun had disappeared almost without warning. Every breath of air had come to a halt and a weary torpor was hanging in the air.

The son found his father sitting on the shoreline. He was minding two lines, one on each side, and holding a third in his hand. He'd seen him coming from a distance and his face softened immediately.

"You look like a professional fisherman," the son exclaimed.

"Well, I do my best. Part of it is the clothes. They have to be made out of the kind of canvas that sailors use. And a big old hat with a brim. But you'd get bored spending hours like this, wouldn't you?"

"I would be bored. Catching fish is fine, but just waiting …"

"But you liked it when you were a boy. I've always loved fishing. It calms me down: when I breathe air like this it feels like I've got the whole sea right in my mouth. I can see the sun set and watch the boats move quietly by. I don't think about anything but at the same time I'm constantly on guard for something exciting to happen. What more do you want? If only life were like that …"

"Any bites?"

"There was a tug on my line just a moment ago that set my heart racing. I thought I'd hooked it, but it got away with half the bait."

"A nice conger?" his son joked, knowing he was touching a nerve. Every kind of eel gave his father the willies: if by some stroke of bad luck he caught one, he would rather lose the line than haul it in.

"Ugh… no. I hope there aren't any eels around here: I tried to choose this spot carefully. I bet it was a big sea bass, one of those old rascals that hang around the port and take your bait in the corner of their mouths and then slip off the hook."

"It's going to be time for supper pretty soon. Aren't you coming to eat?" There was some concern in his son's voice.

"I'll be right along. You go on. I want to see if that old rascal can fool me a second time." His father spoke calmly, his mind completely absorbed with his fishing.

The son left, walking slowly along the bank. Foul odors from inside the houses mixed with the stench of decay given off by certain stagnant zones in the port. He couldn't seem to shake the despondency that had dogged him since early afternoon. Everything made him vaguely nauseous: the thought of returning to that suffocating house, of finding slovenly old Teresa in her dirty dressing gown, the sickly daughter-in-law with her victim's eyes, the seminarian, smarmy like his sweaty hands. Of having to sit back down at the table surrounded by those old relics from an antique bazaar, and constantly worried he was about to see a mouthful get stuck in his father's throat. Of not being able to help him, not even to humor his brave determination to pretend his illness didn't exist.

Seeing him at the edge of the sea just now concentrating so hard on that stupid pastime, he'd forced himself to sound lighthearted, but sadness had welled up within him. Maybe he really didn't know how to treat life lightheartedly and was about to become a burden to his father instead of a consolation: that would render the sacrifice of leaving the mountains completely worthless.

"Your father promised he'd be here for supper tonight," Teresa scolded him. "A sailor's promise! I know these Sunday fishermen. Fortunately, I didn't believe him: for you, a nice veal steak. Would you like that? And for your father I chopped up some meat and dressed it with oil and mustard; that's something I know he would eat with pleasure, just like in the old days."

The table had been set and the widow and the seminarian were already sitting there still and silent. To make conversation, the son asked the young man if they had to study a lot at the seminary. While he was trying to explain the various subjects and how many hours they had to study, excited voices and rapid footsteps rang out on the stairs: it sounded like an argument.

"And he thought he was just toying with me …"

"Unbelievable…"

His father and Teresa rushed into the room. The first thing the son noticed was how his father looked: his face was aglow and pale with emotion.

"Unbelievable, unbelievable," Teresa kept exclaiming, shuffling awkwardly around him as if she were trying to take something away from him that he didn't want to let go of. Even the seminarian had risen to his feet and kept on saying "Magnificent."

The father was holding a huge sea bass in the air; every now and again it would wiggle its silvery tail and struggle for breath by opening its blood red gills.

"I got him this time," his father said turning to his son. "You can see that I knew what I was talking about." His voice and hands were still trembling with emotion.

"I'll bet it weighs two kilos," Teresa announced.

"You take it. I'm going to wash my hands and come right to the table."

Teresa was finally in her element: she hefted and inspected the fish like an expert.

"Two kilos; maybe more. You don't see very many of these big ones: they're a rarity these days. My late husband, poor thing, he would bring me some like this when he went fishing. Always at dusk at this same hour. I'm going to cook it in broth and serve it with mayonnaise for all of you tomorrow. It got here at the perfect time; tomorrow is Sunday and we'll have a special lunch."

His father came back down, still somewhat excited.

"I really feel like eating tonight. Good girl, Teresa, you've fixed me some raw meat."

While he was eating, he answered their questions with an animated story: his protracted struggle with the huge fish, how he had teased it by putting more bait on the hook, with what cunning he had let it take out the line so that it wasn't suspicious and swallowed the bait for sure. Then his hard work and care in pulling it in to the shore, slowly, slowly, taking in line and playing it out, until he had managed to guide it over to the little ladder that led into the sea and then stick his hands into the water and haul it in from there. "That's the last time it's going to break a line on me."

The son was half relieved to see his father talk so animatedly and eat with such gusto and confidence, but he was also half afraid that something was about to happen. He wanted to tell him with every mouthful he took that he should, "Be careful, eat slowly, don't talk." When he could see the empty plate in front of him, he felt he had been liberated from a nightmare.

His father had them open a bottle of vintage wine and insisted that Teresa sit at the table and have a glass with them too.

He had a knack for making unhappy people feel cheerful. Bleak surroundings and glum faces didn't sit well with him; and especially when circumstances had made someone feel bad, he would do all he could to create an atmosphere of cordial affability to make them feel better. His son could remember moving instances of derelicts, of down-and-outers who, in the presence and warmth of his father, were completely transformed, able to bring back to life the happy aspects of their personalities that had been snuffed out by life's adversities.

At that moment, those three human beings buffeted by misfortunes—those three, timorous humans who lived in the shadow of those walls—were no longer recognizable. The good-looking and jovial woman that Teresa must have been was emerging from beneath the crust of the brutal, humiliating neglect of the last few years. The daughter-in-law seemed an actress who'd taken her place at a noisy party without having had time to change out of the widow's weeds she'd worn on stage. And the young man, his mind untethered from his customary priggishness, was moving about naturally, almost as if he were trying to counteract the rigidity of his seminarian's cassock.

Teresa insisted that "in order to better enjoy the wine" everyone had to sample the fritters she'd already prepared for the next day, along with some special grapes she'd had brought in from a tiny nearby island and that were better than any in the whole world. When she came back from the kitchen, she was out of breath but triumphantly bearing a tray with a mound of rubiola grape clusters in the middle and little golden fritters all around them.

"Oh, Teresa, those grapes ... you don't know what memories ..." his father exclaimed.

"I do know, you bet I know, and you should be ashamed of yourself to think about such things in front of your son."

"The little island of love," continued his father undaunted, "where you could exchange kisses under the arbors while the grape clusters quivered between the lovers' lips ..."

"You really are shameless," Teresa cried in delight.

"Too bad the island was so small; certain evenings there was no place to tie up the boat, and you had to make do with a sky with no vine leaves in it and kisses with no grapes."

"Stop it, stop it. Just eat."

It was then, with the first grape that he put in his mouth, that everything went bad. Just as at lunch, his father had to leave unexpectedly. When he came back, the others were in a different mood too.

"Did you feel sick?" asked Teresa.

"A grape got stuck in my throat; hang on, it'll go down," said his father.

"Maybe drink something ..."

"I can't; that's no good right now."

There was a tragic tone in his father's words that his nonchalant air was unable to conceal.

*****

The night brought little rest. Around midnight, the son went out into the hallway and, seeing a sliver of light, went into his father's room.

He was seated on the bed leaning against the pillows and smoking: his gaze steady, the cigarette between his fingers.

"Can't sleep?" his son asked.

"I don't sleep much in general... But what about you?"

"I think it would be better if we leave tomorrow ..."

"Leave? Why?"

"If that grape were to ..."

"I'll get it down. I don't see why we have to leave."

For the first time, there was some resentment in his father's voice.

The son went back out without having had the courage to insist. He was sick at heart—anything might happen and there was nothing he could do to prevent it.

He stood staring out the window for a long time. The memory of the radiology office was still on his mind. His innermost fears were suddenly bathed in a violet light. A slender thread had barely made it past that constriction in his esophagus. "It's not a grape, poor Papa; it's the cancer that's grown bigger and blocked up that narrow passageway too. The grape is just an illusion, maybe the last one." Suddenly and without warning! The doctor's prognosis was coming true. His father was never going to be able to swallow either food or liquids again.

A shiver ran down his spine; and even though the heat was suffocating, the sweat around his waist and on his forehead was cold to the touch. The mosquitos continued to annoy him with their testy buzzing. Avoiding his irritated slaps, they seemed frantically determined to land on and stick tight to all the exposed places on his face.

The water in the port was glittering dark and still, almost sinister. The little garden smelled of rotting plants. Down below, now that the shutters of the café were closed, every sound of life had ceased.

The island appeared marooned at the center of an overwhelming vastness. For the first time, he could feel a strange anguish when he realized that he was all alone, completely cut off from all human interaction.

He stood there listening. On the other side, his father was coughing: a persistent, muffled cough that echoed in his heart. Just like the night before, it was dawn before he was able to fall asleep.

*****

He woke up dispirited, upset, and with his head in a spin. In the room across the hall, maybe his father was exhausted and thinking he was about to die. They needed to leave immediately, that very day. The steamer arrived at noon; barely time to pack the bags; but even without them; the important thing was to leave; he'd have his father carried.

When he opened the shutters, he was blinded and almost driven back inside. The sun was high, sky and sea dazzled like reflecting mirrors. Then his befuddled gaze was attracted by something light-colored on the shore below the house. A little yellow boat with a sparkling white awning was bobbing at the slightest movement made by the boatman sitting at the bow and holding it close to the steps on the bank. The only bit of meager, calming shade in all that dazzling turquoise glare came from the flapping awning.

Turning his gaze elsewhere, the son gave a start, his heart in his mouth. Standing on the bank in the blinding sun not far from the little boat and looking up at him was his father.

"Glad you're up; did you sleep badly?"

"But you … what's going on?" Choked by emotion, the son had difficulty saying anything.

"Today's Sunday. I rented this little boat. It'll take us straight there; and in that way we won't have to go the long way around. I'm going to take you to the Pineta. You wanted to go swimming at the Pineta. Whenever you're ready … I'll be waiting down here at the café."

Once again, the son thought he was dreaming. Pulling back in from the window, he looked at himself in the mirror. He was the sick one: underneath the heathy glow from the mountains his skin was grayish, his eyes had circles under them. His hands trembled visibly while he was shaving. Could his father possibly have gotten up, be standing out there in the sun, waiting to take him for a swim? A moment ago, he had decided he was going to have him carried to the steamer and leave immediately because there was no time to waste.

He washed and dressed in a rush and went down. At that hour, the café was deserted. His father was sitting at a small table; in front of him was a half-empty glass of vermouth. His son could feel his spirits rise: "And so, you are able to drink, the grape ..." he was about to say; but when he looked up into his father's face, the words died on his lips. His face was clenched in brutal pain: frozen, neck muscles taut, his eyes bulging out of their sockets.

He got to his feet, went through the little door into the courtyard, and came back wiping his mouth with his handkerchief.

"No matter what I do, I can't get that damned grape to go down."

"Papa, let's leave right away, this noon."

His father furrowed his brow in surprise and threw him a hostile look.

"There's no reason to leave. This morning we're going to go swimming."

He left a coin on the table. Striding out determinedly, he headed toward the shore, went down the steps, and got into the boat. His son followed him mechanically, disconsolate. Faced with his father's resolve, he felt inadequate.

"Do you want to row? You used to like to," his father said gently, as if he were sorry for the brusque tone he had just used.

His son shook his head.

"Well, then, go on back there," his father said, pointing to the cushioned seat in the stern.

The son decided not to contradict him and tried to make room for his father next to where he was sitting.

"No, the boat wouldn't be balanced properly." And he took his place on the uncomfortable seat in the prow.

The little boat set out, slipping ahead quietly to the slow strokes of the old boatman who'd taken the oars. They crossed through the port. The sun was beating down on the row of houses along the shore, dancing on the expanse of water. There was something frightening and forbidding about the space beneath that glare. The shade provided as if in a dreamy dance by the bright white, fluttering awning was the only thing that dared challenge the implacable atmosphere.

But what sort of cargo was it, underneath that festive awning, in that little yellow boat playing cat and mouse with the jittery reflection it made in the water? The son shuddered at the memory of an awful experience one day in Venice when in the middle of a Grand Canal all pulsing with light and life, he had seen a funeral gondola glide by.

They disembarked on the shore opposite the end of the port. Out there, arching toward the distant and invisible entrance to the inlet, the terrain was rocky and desolate, with scattered junipers and a thicket of conifers in the middle of which a red roof gleamed.

The son had another moment of hesitation. He felt he should try to persuade his father that it was absurd to set off on foot in all that heat, that he needed to see a doctor; he didn't want to go swimming at all. He was uneasy and thinking that the only reasonable thing to do was to go back and then leave.

But his father, after having told the boatman to come pick them up at the same place around noon, had already set off resolutely under the lashing heat.

The road rose higher, then levelled off. Alongside it, the stark landscape was thick with agave plants, some lifting their broad flowered stalks in monstrous astonishment. They passed a couple of villas: the buildings and walls were a jarring note that clashed unnaturally in that solitude.

But on this side the island was completely unprotected, exposed to the northwest wind. Father and son walked side by side in silence. In the intense light, the contours of things vibrated as if electrified; the wind was almost visible as it blew past them, spreading the noise it made everywhere.

The son couldn't muster the courage to look at his father, but he could sense that he was there and could feel almost physically how thirsty he was and what an effort he was making to stay on his feet and march ahead.

At one point the sharply defined shadow his father was making parted company with his own—though up to this point they had flowed together—and this made him feel so sorry for him that his eyes filled with tears. His father was detaching himself from him; in life too he would only be with him for a few days more.

The moment had arrived. Out there on the open road, he had to tell his father everything that had been building up within him for a year now and had often risen to his lips only for him to always choke it back down.

"Papa, you're dying. Here you are walking next to me but your days, maybe your hours, are numbered. Everything we've built up around you has been a pretense; we assumed that what we were doing would provide you with some courage, you who have so much more of that than we do. The doctor was lying from the very first day when he told you that your illness could be cured, that all you needed to do was hold on. I was lying in what I said to you, the way I behaved, and how I held out false hopes; I've been lying to you right up to this very moment ...

"You have cancer, and you don't get well from cancer. It's not a grape that's stuck in your esophagus—it's swollen tissue. You won't be able to eat or drink any more. Death, which has been looming over you all this time, has now bent down to put a hand on your shoulder and will soon be ready to push your head down with the other hand and then to carry you off clasped in its arms. It's not right for me to keep on with this comedy ....

"Though maybe both of us are doing this. You know the truth, don't you Papa? Maybe you're not saying anything so as not to frighten me. If that's the case, let's tear off our masks. That would be more like us, more like you who has always taught me to face reality head on. These few hours—the final ones—that we agreed to spend together, let's not waste them. It's not my going for a swim, it's not this brilliant sunny morning that matter ...

"Maybe you've been waiting for me to say all this. You need to get ready to die, to know that someone who has the same blood in his veins as you do is standing right next to you. So here I am. It's not the world with its twisted objects and images that's alongside you now: it's me who's listening to you and understands you and isn't keeping anything from you ... Say something, Papa, you can open up completely, accept the dreadful weight that is hanging on your heart, get matters finally under control. I'll be right here ready to help you shoulder the burden."

Right in the center of all that light, a ghastly vision suddenly appeared before the son's dazed eyes. His father was walking next to him, lifeless, a white skeleton with arms extended carrying its heart in its hands; the black shadow was exactly like the one he was casting onto the roadway. Horrible. The lump in his throat was making him choke. No, he wouldn't be able to say a word.

Silence, their mechanical footsteps, the monstrous agave plants, the wind, the sea in the background, the immensity of the sky: everything out on that road had a part to play in the tragedy.

*****

They went on walking in silence. A noise from behind them made them turn around. Two girls on bikes went by; their bright-colored bathing suits and graceful movements hung in the air with all the exuberance of life; their happy voices were carried to them for a long time by the rush of the wind. Then they disappeared from view.

The road was empty once more. This road leading straight toward the infinite blue of the sea and sky; uninhabited, with a few boarded up, apparently vacant houses alongside it, and here and there, sterile masses of stones and gravel. Smooth and unvarying, stretching out silent and compact underfoot, it was dominating all their thoughts and feelings like some relentless destiny.

But maybe what the son had wanted to say to his father earlier was inhumane. Maybe he needed to take the opposite tack and go halfway, matching his generosity with some of his own, making him happy, distracting him.

"Life, Papa, leaves such a brief taste in your mouth, though what a rich one! It's like this wind that smells of the sea: all you have to do is breathe it in. You saw those two girls a moment ago: they were heading straight into the delicious nothingness that constitutes life and doing so with utter joy. How the island quivers with air and sky here: a little nest of rocks in the midst of immensity, but how it pulsates in the sun, how the wind delights it. I think of our ancestors' ships when they came back from distant lands and seas and were about to arrive at the tiny spot where they had been born. How excited they must have been to see its silhouette, its rocks glistening with salt. And Grandpa? I can see his bright blue eyes begin to squint as his lips break into that satisfied, rascally grin of his."

This is what would have made his father smile and forget about his own anguish and start to talk about the high-masted ships, the prevailing winds, his own father, his voyages back home.

But another specter had begun to unsettle his thoughts. Beneath that pitiless glare, it was no longer two men walking down a road but a pair of clowns. One of them dead and the other alive, strolling along in buffoonish camaraderie, they were each wearing the same kind of mask and chatting cheerfully and then, when conversation would flag, jingling the bells attached to their sleeves and hats.

Once again, the son didn't know what to say. A heavy, tense silence was weighing on them. Which of the two would open his mouth first? Would it be possible to dispel the weighty barrier of that silence with the triviality of a commonplace, some shallow phrase?

His father was gloomily aware that his whole organism was struggling with the damned grape that was starting to ruin even the few days he'd been promising himself he would enjoy on the island with his son. He was exasperated by his carelessness and vowed that if he ever managed to free himself from that blockage, he would never again risk having to die from hunger, just for the sake of some stupid gluttony.

He'd expel the blockage, of course he would, never mind how he had failed to do so up to now. His muscles and nerves were still solid and willing. He was putting them to the test out on that road: his pace was elastic, his body holding up just fine. Except that thirst was starting to drive him crazy: an all-encompassing thirst that he seemed to feel not just in his throat but in his stomach and intestines and all through his veins. That's why the sea breeze blowing toward him was such a liberation: he breathed in the damp salty air, drinking it in through every pore.

Every now and again he stole a glance at his son; he could see how sad and miserable he looked. Why did he want to leave? He should have been thinking about enjoying himself. He was an extremely healthy young man at that happy age when all you have to do is stretch out your hand to pluck life's richest fruits.

He was about to say to him, "Don't worry so much about me, this old man who's come to an end. Obey your instincts. Just look at this morning and the swim that it's getting ready for you. Your gloominess is making me gloomy, while I would be happy if you were too. I've always prided myself on having passed my cheerful character on to you. If it's starting to be snuffed out in me, let me have the satisfaction of seeing it sparkle in you. Yesterday morning it made me feel happy ..."

Without warning, the road had reached its highest point and an incredible spectacle lay before the two men who, almost as if by one accord, came to a halt.

Below them, a thick wreath of soft vegetation, airy and waving, crowned a broad inlet in a perfect semicircle around whose golden sand an amethyst sea of enchanting transparency was rocking gently before curling into sprightly foam as it washed ashore. The whole grove was quivering with the inebriated sound of the cicadas competing with the booming rhythm of the sea.

Every once and a while, fleeting sounds of human voices arose above that powerful chorus before being dispersed by the wind. The resort, with its jetties and bright-colored bathing huts, its shining waters flecked with bathers whose heads looked like so many pumpkins, seemed like a toy that had been carelessly cast up there by the waves.

For the first time, father and son looked each other in the face and, forgetting about themselves, were able to dredge honest smiles up out of their melancholy, and began to talk to each other, saying how delighted they were with the spectacle that lay before them.

*****

But once they started back, the son was overcome by dread once again. He hadn't wanted to go swimming. He'd rather have stayed with his father on the terrace of the resort, but he knew his father would have been annoyed by the idea and so he didn't even bring it up.

In other circumstances, he'd have truly enjoyed the fragrant cool of the sea in the shade of the bathing hut, but now it gave him no pleasure. He undressed mechanically. All those nude bodies on the boardwalk, those glistening torsos emerging from the water, that noisy promiscuity of men and women, that mixing of shapes and of young and old flesh, all without any sense of decorum: that vision gave made him feel that he was looking at a nest of worms, of swarming undifferentiated life.

How much better that swim the other morning when he was all alone and in direct contact with the elements of nature! Not one bit of what they had seen from above a moment earlier was a part of that swarm. So in order to recapture that, at least in part, he swam with bold strokes out to the open sea. Once he knew he was far from shore, he turned onto his back and paddled toward the pine grove. That expanse of soft emerald foliage, waving in the wind and resonant with the sound of the cicadas, made him feel that he had arrived, after a difficult pilgrimage, at a land of peace and contemplation.

It only lasted a moment. He couldn't relax, wasn't able to enjoy himself while his father, not far away, was struggling in the grip of a terrible future.

He swam back, got out of the water, and dressed while still damp. Concerned, he climbed the steps to the terrace. His father wasn't expecting him back so soon. He was sitting in the far corner of the terrace with a big glass of ice-cold lemonade in his hand.

His son felt torn by compassion for him. "He keeps right on trying," he thought, when he saw him lean over the rail and spit out the bit of liquid that he had in his mouth.

Turning then to his son, the father tried to control the dark thoughts that were churning on his face. He shook his head but didn't attempt a smile. Utter sadness had settled over his features. He motioned toward the glass that he'd set down on the rail.

"Just wanted to cool my mouth off."

How many futile attempts, how many setbacks he must have had in the short time he'd been up there by himself before coming up with that lie.

"It's early. Sit down with me for a while. Were you the one swimming way out there? I thought so. You know, it used to be that all the ships, whether they were leaving or returning to the island, would pass by just beyond this inlet. People would come here to wave white handkerchiefs in last goodbyes or first welcomes home. Some captains, coming back after long voyages, would heave to and send the dingy to shore to pick up family members and take them on board so that they could arrive in port together a couple of hours later. When I was a boy, it was my greatest thrill when my father would send for us. After they had been gone so many months, everything on the ship seemed new to us. My father would be waiting for us in his cabin and his presents from America or the Indies would be spread out on his table."

His father was talking calmly. With the open gulf lying before him, memories of a life lived justly and in good health were pouring out of him like amazing revelations he was eager to share: lives like these were the island's most important heritage. Now and then he would start to cough, and his voice had grown raspy, though softened by an enormous gentleness.

"Did grandfather die young?"

"Yes, he did. I was barely fourteen. Women are the ones who live on; men from here either die or wear out first."

The racket made by the bathers was continuing down below them; there still wasn't anyone else on the broad terrace, but the waiters were already setting the tables for lunch.

"In those days," his father went on, "this resort wasn't here; neither were the houses that you see scattered through the pine grove. The place was a wilderness; the thicket of trees was denser and the sound of the cicadas in the summer was even more deafening. To me this little inlet seemed like one vast, infinite gulf, the biggest gulf in the whole world."

*****

The walk back was extremely taxing. From time to time, his father was racked by a hacking cough; his mouth was entirely dry and he must have been increasingly tormented by thirst. He seemed calm and was trying to carry on a conversation, but there was already a sense of hopeless exhaustion in his voice. The light in his eyes had gone out. His legs were wobbly.

"If only I could help him!" Was there anything he could do for his father at this moment? Nothing. His son was growing increasingly anxious. At least get back to Teresa's house right away. But after that? The idea of what would happen afterwards filled him with horror. Leaving meant holding out until the afternoon, sticking it out until night; the next steamer wasn't due until ten o'clock the next day; the crossing was a long one. His sense of helplessness exasperated him. The endless road beneath the scorching sun was turning into a nightmare.

When they finally got to the landing, the sight of the boat waiting for them there was a bit of a relief. His father hesitated a moment before putting his foot on board. His son took him by the arm and helped him to sit down on the cushioned seat in the stern; his body was trembling slightly.

It had been too much for him! There was nothing that alarmed his son more than his father's resignation.

The slow regularity with which the boatman rowed was like a metronome, like life throbbing on, indifferent to any need for haste, any sense of personal suffering.

"I've been unfair to you, making you come down to this furnace from up where it was cool. But it won't be long before you can go back to your mountains again."

The only way the son could have responded to his father's words would have been with tears, asking for forgiveness that he hadn't been able to be more cheerful.

At the house, Teresa welcomed them gaily.

"I've made some mayonnaise for your fish; you've never tasted anything like it."

She became confused and was disappointed when she had to accept—and this wasn't easy for her—that the father didn't feel well and wasn't going to have anything to eat.

"You, though, go ahead and eat," he said to his son once he had taken him to his room. There was still a trace of energy in his voice.

At the big midday meal, the son felt dazed: all that would come to his imagination was the road with the gloomy agave plants and the image of his father. He ate so little that Teresa was worried and came out of the kitchen to complain that it served her right, that she shouldn't ever bend over backwards for other people, that she had no idea what was going on.

The son tried to calm her down, saying that his father's illness was very serious: the next day they were going to have to leave. But meanwhile he was going to ask the doctor what he could do to help the sick old man; he asked her please not to disturb him.

*****

They had him wait in a parlor whose walls were covered with photographs and that was jammed with chairs of various sizes smelling of dust and age. The trunk of a palm tree behind the house made it impossible for air and light to get through the single window half-hidden by moth-eaten velvet curtains. The room was suffocating. The son knew he couldn't stand it for long in there: he really was at the end of his rope.

The doctor, short and fat, came into the room in shirtsleeves and with his trousers loosened. His eyes were clouded over, and he looked like he was suffering from indigestion.

As he listened to himself talk, the son could feel that suddenly he was tearing away the thin layer of emotions that up to that point had encased him. There was something cruel about the way he explained his father's situation to the doctor. With blunt objectivity, he described the X-ray he'd observed: that esophagus with the constriction at the third rib could just as well have been someone else's esophagus. The grape that his father had struggled with so bravely became just another detail, one without any psychological importance.

The doctor listened to him; then he plopped down onto an armchair, setting off a sour stench of dust as he did so.

It was certainly possible that a foreign body had hastened the constriction. Operate? Try to push it down or open up a passageway? Yes, some probing could be attempted. But it was a delicate affair. He couldn't guarantee that he wouldn't rupture an artery, maybe even the aorta: who knows what the cancer had done to the tissues. The only option was gastrostomy, which would allow him to be nourished directly through his stomach: one incision and then a feeding tube. He could perform such an operation himself, if necessary, right on the island; but there was enough time to take him back to the city. Didn't he really think it better to have him operated on in the city? Fine. There was no need for him to examine him. Until it came time for them to get on the boat, he should lie down so as not to waste energy; meanwhile, to combat the dryness, he should keep a piece of ice in his mouth. He knew who his father was: true island stock. He'd never have suspected that he might get cancer; it truly pained him: a man who might have lived to be ninety. But this was how things were: men from the island rarely made it beyond sixty.

"Where I come from, men either die or wear out first": how calm his father's voice had been on the terrace! For the son, that moment—such a short time ago—seemed to be something from the distant past. Up until that moment, a sense of tragedy had been dominating his thoughts, and he was still torn between despair and hope; afterwards, everything, even suffering, seemed to have degenerated into something lackluster and inevitable. As far as he was concerned, his father was already dead: the axe of destiny had severed the old root from the young, still living trunk. He could feel the pain, but it felt like a wound that will scab over and not a diseased body part through which family blood is circulating. The image of the doctor, the airless room, the miserable little garden stretching beyond the house, the port dazzled by the sun, the island itself were all rushing toward him, coalescing into a depiction of life in the provinces where everything that happens is reduced to a common denominator of mediocrity. Suddenly, he felt homesick for the high mountains.

He bought their tickets at the agency and reserved a cabin on the first possible steamer. When he was about to enter his father's room, he started to worry that once again he might refuse to leave. If that turned out to be the case, he was going to go back and ask the doctor to come and persuade him.

The look his father gave him from the bed when he heard him come in was powerful enough to turn his thoughts topsy-turvy. The iciness he felt within him quickly gave way to a burning sense of remorse. His father was no more than a defenseless creature, helpless in his terrified resignation in the face of the cruelest of blows. Everyone was free to strike out at him, with the worst abuse of all maybe coming from his own flesh and blood.

"Oh, father," he'd have liked to cry out, "why did you pick such a difficult moment to ask for help from a person who isn't worthy or capable of providing it?" He should have said something to him, the way he'd wanted to while out on the road to the Pineta, something to lift up his spirits and make him feel better. Now it was too late. The physical support that he could provide was cruel rather than consoling.

"We have to leave as soon as we can. I've had a talk with the doctor. You need to have a minor operation: it's better to have it done in the city."

His lying was inevitable by now, with no way to not keep on with it right up to the end.

His father lowered his head and then was wracked by a lengthy fit of coughing; his eyes were watering and his forehead damp with perspiration.

The room was filled with smoke.

"You shouldn't smoke anymore; it dries up your saliva. They'll bring you some ice now."

His father didn't object or respond. A resigned sadness had settled over him. The son could feel a sense of emptiness, the beginnings of bad feelings between him and his father. His discomfort was growing, changing into a nervous desire to run away. But, abruptly, he went over and sat on the edge of the bed.

"Are you unhappy, Papa?"

"I thought I'd be braver. You never really know who you are."

His son's heart leapt in his chest; he had begun to glimpse a ray of light. There it was. He still had time to talk to him: the truth would make both of them feel better.

"Do me a favor," his father continued. "See that box on the table. The line that I used yesterday afternoon to catch that sea bass must be there too. Put it back with the rest of the tackle."

*****

Clustered in the little square around the marble bust of the famous baritone, the band that performed every Sunday played until late in the evening. The seaside was teeming with people: islanders and tourists strolled by the café, which had set out lots of tables. Once the band stopped, you could hear footsteps on the cobblestones and the conversations of people who were having a drink or eating ice cream.

The mosquitos, attracted in clouds by the streetlamps on the waterfront, were pouring into the dark bedroom once again. There the son, in the grips of an uneasy stupor, was seated in the armchair listening to see if his help was needed across the hallway.

He sat there quietly, lifting a cautious hand only when some of the many mosquitos buzzing around him lit on his neck or face: he had caught on by now how to squash them.

Just beyond, his father was still coughing. Perceptible above the drums and brass of the band, above the racket of the festivities, that cough had a resonance that made every other sound seem trivial. This was a man who had already stepped out of the current of life and now was standing on the shore, tarrying there a bit before disappearing. With that echoing cough he was sending a terrible warning to everyone, never mind whether they knew what to make of it.

On certain nights, he had heard a similar sound in the calm of the mountains. It was a roebuck barking. Pain, fear? Maybe it was being pursued by hunters and so the barking was a harbinger of imminent death? Why is it that people, who try to make sense of everything, pay so little attention to the animal in them, the animal that is a part of every living creature?

Once the carousing had come to an end, the son went repeatedly into the hallway and crept over to the door to the other room. Though the light was on, there was no telling what his father might be doing in those moments. He wasn't sleeping; with that cough, sleep would have been impossible. Could he have been thinking, his eyes fixed and his face a tragic mask, about his imminent death? Was he reading his *Bible*, his glasses bouncing up and down on his nose every time he had to cough? Was he dreaming of feeling a big fish tugging on his fishing line, "the one that got away," but that this time was not as clever as he was? Or was he re-living his past life? How many events, how many joys, what a wealth of passionate life made up that past! But now, nothing except the incessant cough, the constant menace of that cough.

As the night began to wane, the son, who had been dozing in the armchair, gazed out the window at the spectacle made by the dawn. The inert expanse of the sea began to tremble and became visible through the haze. The houses of the little town all huddled around the port were still snuggling half asleep in the soft light, when all at once they were shaken awake by a burning river of light spilling down on top of them: the sun had suddenly risen. The son closed his eyes, and a slow shiver ran through his whole body: he felt like he was the one who had been abandoned and was going to die, he was the one who was suffering.

He found his father propped up on the pillows, with a cigarette in his fingers. He still had the determination and strength to keep on smoking. The night had marked his face with deep fatigue, but in his dull eyes and somewhat ironic mouth there were signs of resolute determination.

"Don't even think about having me carried to the steamer. I'll get there on my own two legs."

He got out of bed so that he could shave, making up for his initial stumbles by holding onto the bedstead.

"Listen now, give me your arm when we go to the steamer: you can be 'the walking stick of my old age.' "

That was the father he'd always known. Rising above the humiliation of this latest trick of fate. This is the way he was going to die, still the person he had always been, still maintaining a sense of confident superiority, stronger than anything that might lie in store for him. This was the truth that mattered to him, the bedrock on which he stood: everything else, including all the falsehoods of those last months, had receded into the background.

On the steamer, the father insisted on staying on deck to say goodbye to his island: then he went down into the cabin.

The son watched the island grow smaller, disappear at the horizon in the immense brilliance of the sea. It was the first time he had ever realized, pure and simple, what he was losing in losing his father.

Books published by Agincourt Press

Michela Dall'Aglio, *In the Beginning There Was Freedom. An Itinerary between Science, Philosophy, and Faith* (2020)

Mariano Bàino, *Yellow Fax and Other Poems* (2019)

Alfredo Giuliani (ed.), *I Novissimi* (2017)

Gianluca Rizzo (ed.), *On the Fringe of the Neoavantgarde / Ai confine della neoavanguardia, Palermo 1963 – Los Angeles 2013* (2017)

Massimo Ciavolella and Gianluca Rizzo (ed.), *Savage Words: Invectives as a Literary Genre* (2016)

Massimo Ciavolella and Gianluca Rizzo (ed.), *Like Doves Summoned by Desire: Dante's New Life in 20th Century Literature and Cinema. Essays in memory of Amilcare Iannucci* (2012)

Elio Pagliarani, *The Girl Carla and Other Poems* (2009)

Maurizio Cucchi, *The Missing* (2008)

Remo Bodei, *We, The Divided: Ethos, Politics, and Culture in Post-War Italy, 1943-2006* (2006)

Standard Shaefer, *Water & Power* (2005)

Robert Crosson, *The Day Sam Goldwyn Stepped off the Train* (2004)

Paul Vangelisti, *Embarrassment of Survival* (2001)